DEAD TIME IN DEADWOOD

JOHN A. RUSSO

Burning Bulb

PUBLISHING

DEAD TIME IN DEADWOOD
by **John A. Russo**

Burning Bulb Publishing
P.O. Box 4721
Bridgeport, WV 26330-4721
www.BurningBulbPublishing.com

Cover designed by Gary Lee Vincent.

First edition.

Paperback edition ISBN 978-1-964172-13-2

AUTHOR'S NOTE: It is a known fact that Heck Thomas, Doc Holliday, Wild Bill Hickok, Wyatt Earp and Calamity Jane were in Deadwood, South Dakota in 1876, however as to what they were doing there at that time, I can only report what I was told by an anonymous source.

CHAPTER 1

On a brutally hot day in July, 1876, Deputy Heck Thomas dismounted by a sparkling stream in a patch of woods and let his horse drink. He had been in the saddle for three hours and now he was in the area twenty miles north of Deadwood, South Dakota, where he was intending to find out whether or not he had been sent on a fool's errand by Sheriff Dylan Parkman.

His tan trousers and denim shirt were soaked with sweat. His entire body felt wet and damp, especially under the leather ammo belt and holster holding his heavy Colt six-gun. He didn't dare to be all alone out here unless he was well armed. His lever-action rifle was in a sheathe tied to his horse's saddle.

He knelt, scooped crystal-clear water into his Stetson, and drank his fill, then splashed water on his sweaty face. He put his soaked hat back on his head and wiped his mouth and chin with the tails of his yellow bandana.

Suddenly he heard shambling footsteps from deep in the patch of woods. He squinted sharply in that direction, alerted to some hissing and rasping sounds and yanked his revolver from its holster.

The ominous sounds stopped.

He called out gruffly, "Whoever you are, show your damned self! Step out where I can see you -- with your hands up!"

Dead silence.

Heck cautiously took a few steps into the woods, twigs and pine needles crackling under his boots, his six-shooter pointed ahead of himself, his finger on the trigger. At first, he saw and heard nothing more. But suddenly he heard rasping breaths -- seeming to come from deeper and darker foliage.

His eyes darting, he caught a glimpse of two shadowy figures seemingly trying to elude him, and he almost squeezed his trigger. But he realized he did not know who or what they were, so he hesitated.

He shrugged but remained on edge and didn't holster his gun till he got back on his horse. Had he seen the two shadowy figures or not? He was no longer completely certain they were a reality. Maybe his mind was addled from heat and exhaustion. Yet logic told him that there wasn't enough wind to rustle leaves and branches, thereby creating the illusion that someone or something was moving back there.

"Buck up," he told himself. And he rode another three or four miles with the sun beating down on him and his black-and-white mare, Susanna, both of them suffering in the scorching heat. He felt guilty that he had chosen to be out here and the horse hadn't but was taken here anyway. He didn't always accept the tasks Sheriff Parkman talked him into, and he thought maybe he should've refused this time.

Finally, he sighted the Brewster family's sod house. Sheriff Parkman had sent him to this godforsaken territory to make sure they were still alive. But now, a feeling of dread came over him because even at a distance, he could see that there were no horses in the corral, and a wagon parked near the dismal sod house had a dead horse hitched to it, and its tongue was lying in the dirt.

As Susanna trotted closer, Heck didn't see or hear any chickens running around clucking, and there weren't any sheep in their pen under a clump of trees. It was as if everything that normally would have been here had been spirited away, leaving nothing but brown earth baked so hard it had cracks in it, yet was still sending up puffs of dust even though there was barely any wind.

Heck felt an impulse to make a fast getaway, but he suppressed it. These days, he was known as one of the toughest lawmen in Deadwood, but he was keenly aware that he had first been toughened up as a twelve-year-old courier in the Civil War, where he had seen bodies torn apart and grown men dying in agony and screaming for their mamas.

He had always given the Brewster family a heap of credit for braving all the potential disasters out here while trying to build a dream based on back-breaking hard work -- but when he spotted four bodies lying in the dirt near the sod house, he knew that their dream must have turned into a nightmare. They must have been raided. Their sheep and chickens were probably cooked, eaten or driven into the wilderness by renegade Indians punishing white settlers for killing off the buffalo herds.

Heck drew his gun, then dismounted and dropped the reins.

He moved closer to one of the dead bodies -- and stopped in his tracks when he saw that it was Caleb Brewster's wife, Abigail. He didn't easily recognize her because part of her face had been ripped away. Her threadbare cotton sleeping gown was torn open in several places, especially around her torso, where there were bloody masses of flesh where her breasts used to be.

Heck mumbled to himself, "What the hell? Coyote? Mountain lion?"

But could a pack of wild carnivores have scared away all of the farm animals they hadn't outright killed?

Suddenly, Abigail Brewster emitted a hissing sigh that was almost a growl. Leaping at Heck with eyes that looked vacant, she clutched at him, trying to bite into his neck.

BLAM! He shot her in her head.

She rasped and gurgled, sank back onto the sun-baked earth, and lay still.

Staring down at her in total shock, Heck slowly got his feet under him -- but then he heard more rasping sounds.

The other three dead bodies also began to come alive -- and the one nearest Heck was a ten-year-old child holding a rag doll.

"Oh, honey," he said ever so softly.

She was little Letty Brewster, who had sat on his lap about three months ago after he gave her hardtack candy from town. He trembled and backed away from her. But when the other two beings shambled toward him, hissing and rasping and baring their teeth, he fired first at the two adults, even though the little girl was closer to him.

The two he shot first, Letty's father and older brother, were on the ground, trying to crawl -- and he realized he had to shoot Letty even if he didn't want to. He shot her in her head, and she fell on her face in the dusty earth, with her rag doll lying partway under her body.

In utter despair, Heck yelled, "What *are* you, goddamn it!"

He backed toward Susanna, seizing her reins and casting wary looks all around. When he was mounted once more, he took time to re-load his gun from the beltful of cartridges around his waist.

CHAPTER 2

On his way back to Deadwood, Heck Thomas stopped at a U.S. Army Trading Post about seven miles from where the Brewster family had been massacred. He knew Sergeant Emmitt Foster, who was in charge of the trading post, because he and Emmitt had once worked together as scouts for General Crook. He knocked on the door frame of the sergeant's office and said, "I've gotta talk with you in private, Emmitt."

"Come in and shut the door," Emmitt said. "Take a seat."

The office was ten feet by twelve feet, its chinked log walls unadorned except for army bulletins and a couple of wanted posters. Sergeant Foster, who rose from behind his plank desk to shake hands with Heck, was a short, blonde fellow with bright yellow suspenders stretched over his blue shirt and pot belly.

Heck sat in one of the two rough-hewn wooden chairs in front of the desk and bluntly said, "I've just come from the Brewster place, and they're all dead, killed in a raid of some sort. I scarcely believe what I have to tell you, Emmitt, but it looked to me like they'd been cannibalized."

"Are you sure?"

"I'm sayin' that's what it looked like. I'd like you to send out a burial party as soon as you can. But use troopers who can be trusted to keep their mouths shut. We don't want the ranchers around here to form a mob that'll kill Lakota women and children. We need time to find out what's really goin' on. I'm sure Sheriff Parkman will be thinking that same way."

"No doubt," Sergeant Foster said grimly. He tugged on his ragged blonde mustache, then said, "Heck, in all seriousness, we both know how the Sioux and the Lakota like to mutilate the dead bodies of their enemies, 'cause they think that'll make 'em so ugly they won't be allowed into the Happy Hunting Ground."

"Right," said Heck. "They also do it to try to scare the white settlers from taking their land."

"But you used the word *cannibalized*, Heck. That's a new one on us both, isn't it? I never heard of it being done before."

"Well, I can only tell you that's what it looked like."

"Okay, but it has to be kept quiet for now," Sergeant Foster said. "If it turns out to be true, and if the Lakota did it, they're gonna have an all-out war on their hands. It'll be worse than Little Big Horn -- but us whites will win this time, that's for *damn* sure!"

CHAPTER 3

Heck had camped overnight during the first two days of his trip to the Brewster place, and he was going to do the same thing on his way back, because seven miles per day was a humane pace to put a horse through in such a debilitating heat spell.

He was glad he hadn't signed up as a scout for General Crook back in March when a thousand troops under his command were sent out to punish the Sioux for the massacre of George Custer's Seventh Cavalry at Little Big Horn. But Crook's troops were short on rations and the newer recruits weren't adequately trained, and on their march toward the Black Hills they were hit with torrential rainfall that caused their expedition to be nicknamed "the mud march." And then it became "the horsemeat march" when the troopers ran out of food and were forced to butcher and eat their own horses.

Heck Thomas learned about the horrors that Crook's men had endured from a detachment sent by Crook to pick up a trainload of emergency supplies in Deadwood. On their way back to their starving comrades, the detachment stumbled upon an encampment of Lakota men, women, and children and opened fire on them. It became known as the Battle of Slim Buttes, one of the largest battles that ever took place on the plains. Crook's troops killed thirty-seven warriors and seized a supply of dried meat that the Indians had stockpiled.

These days, Heck sympathized with the guys in the blue uniforms, whereas when he was a boy, they were the hated "blue bellies" who had invaded his homeland. Yet, he had learned back then that there could be such a thing as gallantry under fire and that, at times, it could outshine the fear and misery of a bloodthirsty war.

One night, when he and several dark-skinned slaves were guarding his uncle Ed's baggage behind the front lines of an ongoing battle, an old man in butternut gray appeared out of the near-darkness carrying a sheathed sword and leading a black horse saddled and bridled but with no rider. The grizzled old soldier said, "I think you're your uncle Ed's courier, little Henry Thomas, am I correct?" And Heck said he was.

The soldier told him, "This horse and sword belonged to a Union officer who's been killed, General Philip Kearny. General Lee wants them delivered through the lines to General Kearny's widow under a flag of truce. General Lee wants me to bring you to him so he can ask you if you are game to accept this mission and judge whether you are the right person to carry it out."

In his high-pitched little-boy voice, Heck stammered, "Gen'ral Lee wants *me?*" He wanted to pinch himself when he stood before the exalted commander of the Army of the Confederacy and took on the mission that Lee wanted him to perform. It was the proudest moment of his life, even now, long after the Southern cause was lost. He fervently believed he would've followed General Lee into the fires of hell, but as things turned out, he came down with Yellow Fever two years prior to Lee's surrender at Appomattox, and was carted back to his family in Athens, Georgia. He spent the last two years of the war slowly getting his health back and working as a clerk in his brother's general store. But by his late teens, hale and hearty again, that job was too tame for him, and his brother used his political pull to get Heck hired onto the Atlanta police force.

In 1876, at age twenty-three, Heck was married and had two young children, and they were living in Fort Worth, Texas, where he had been hired as a railroad detective. He was so successful at putting train robbers behind bars that Judge Isaac Parker, the so-called "hanging judge" of Fort Smith, Arkansas, sought him out and swore him in as a United States Deputy Marshal. He was chasing outlaws all through Indian Territory, killing some of them and putting the rest in shackles, when Sheriff Dylan Parkman petitioned Judge Parker for the use of Heck's services in Deadwood, South Dakota, which didn't even exist till a few years before Heck got there.

Deadwood began as an encroachment on land granted to the Lakota people in the 1868 Treaty of Fort Laramie. The Black Hills were sacred to them, and they hated the white settlers who violated the treaty. The situation went from bad to worse in 1874 when an expedition led by Lieutenant Colonel George Armstrong Custer discovered gold on French Creek. The Black Hills Gold Rush was on, and miners, scammers, and profit-seekers of every stripe swelled the lawless town from a few hundred recluses to over five thousand reckless adventurers, and they all had needs of the flesh that must be met. Realizing it, two rugged entrepreneurs, Charlie and Steve Utter, led a wagon train full of eagerly sought commodities and luxuries into Deadwood, not just bars of soap and tons of dry goods but also prostitutes. Madame Mustache and Dirty Em immediately set up thriving brothels catering to the gamblers, gold miners, and gunslingers.

Heck's young wife knew all of this all too well, so when he took leave of her and their two toddlers, he had to promise her not to stay on the job in Deadwood for longer than sixty days and to come home to Fort Smith sooner if the job got done quicker. The main incentive for both of them was that Sheriff Parkman was going to pay him twice the money he was making under Judge Isaac Parker, and Parkman could well afford to do so because the town's treasury was bulging with money from the gold mines.

When Heck first got back to town, just after nightfall, he checked into his room at the Golden Nugget Hotel for a hot bath and a good night's sleep, then hit the sack so totally worn out mentally and physically that he was dead to the world.

In the morning, with his horse, Susanna, being fed and curried at a livery stable, Heck walked the short distance from the hotel to the sheriff's office, which was housed in a log building adjacent to the town jail. Sheriff Parkman wasn't expecting him and was so startled to all of a sudden see him that he jerked around and made hot coffee dribble down his chin.

"Shit! That burns!" the sheriff yipped. "Damn it, Heck, did you have to burst in on me like that?" He wiped his mouth and chin with the heel of his hand, then rubbed the wetness on his denim trousers.

Sheriff Parkman was tall and hefty, about fifty pounds heavier than Heck was, and twenty years older, and his thick hair and handlebar mustache had gone completely gray. He had been a U.S. Marshal before getting elected as Deadwood's sheriff, and he and Heck shared a bond that came from sometimes working as a team in pursuit of vicious desperadoes. They were both part of a large posse that gunned down Ed Reed, Belle Starr's first husband, after he killed a rancher and went on the run.

But Heck and the sheriff both knew Heck wasn't there to chit-chat about old times. They stood facing each other across the sheriff's desk, which was a plank sitting on top of two barrels, and Heck said, "It's worse than we feared, Dylan. I was attacked by four of 'em -- dead human beings that somehow aren't dead and aren't even human anymore."

"Who were they before they got that way?" the sheriff immediately wanted to know.

He already knew enough about the strange situation he and Heck were facing that he was sure Heck wasn't spewing nonsense.

"It was the whole Brewster family -- or what *used* to be them," Heck said. "I recognized 'em, but could hardly believe my own eyes. And what's more, before I even got to their sheep farm, I almost got attacked by what was likely a couple more just like them while I was watering my horse, but they sneaked off into the woods."

"Holy hell! Who were *they* do you think?"

"Don't know. I never got a good look."

"Whites or Injuns?"

"I didn't catch enough of a glimpse."

"Who knows about any of this?" the sheriff asked.

"So far, just you and me."

Sheriff Parkman sighed and sank heavily into the chair behind his plank desk, plunking is tin cup down so hard that coffee slurped out.

Heck said, "We can't keep a lid on it for very long, whether folks panic nor not. They've gotta know what's up so they can protect themselves and their families. Especially the homesteaders who are out there isolated."

"But we can't tell them much because we really don't know what the hell's goin' on," said the sheriff. "I don't have a glimmer. Do you?"

Heck mulled it over, then said, "You ask me, I think it's tied in with that stupid Ghost Dance the Injuns are all hopped up on. They think their ancestors are gonna come outta their graves and destroy all us white people and give 'em their land back with all the millions of buffalo that used to be on it."

Sheriff Parkman said, "It's that Injun soothsayer, Nocona. He's the fanatic fillin' their heads with that crap. I want you to find him and bring him back here in chains. I'll charge him with inciting the murders of the Brewster family and I'll make him think he's gonna hang unless he can prove he had nothing to do with it. Maybe he'll point his finger at some of his disciples, as he calls them."

Heck said, "You want me to go into Lakota territory all alone? I ain't partial to gettin' myself skinned alive, Dylan."

"I know you'll need backup. I'm gonna deputize Billy Hickok to go with you. He's a wild sumbitch but he don't take no shit from nobody. He's quick on the draw. He has an itchy trigger finger but when he shoots he don't miss."

"Yeah, Wild Bill Hickok, that's what they call him, and he's proud of it," said Heck. "Didn't he up and marry that woman who used to be a scout for Custer? She's a prostitute, I think, or she used to be, but that didn't stop him. She calls herself Calamity Jane 'cause she says any man who crosses her is courtin' a calamity."

Sheriff Parkman chuckled. He said, "I could easily believe that, Heck. She might be just the kind of woman who can keep Billy Hickok in line."

CHAPTER 4

Dylan Parkman and Heck Thomas walked from the sheriff's office to the Golden Nugget Hotel, where they ordered the Deluxe $2.25 breakfast at the restaurant on the first floor of the new six-story redbrick building, one of the grandest in Deadwood, and almost as gaudy as the Victorian-style brothels. The lawmen were served big oval-shaped platters of eggs, sausages, bacon, grits, and thick slices of toasted homemade bread with as much freshly churned butter and maple syrup as they craved -- and after four days of eating only beans on the trail, Heck craved plenty.

After they ate their fill, they leaned back, patted their stomachs, and relaxed with cups full of freshly topped-off coffee, and the sheriff said, "To get back into a distasteful subject, near the end of last week, just after you headed out, I received a packet from the government in Washington, which turned out to be a twenty-page report from the Department of the Interior, expressing great fear of what the Ghost Dancing thing is doin' to the Lakota. Particularly the warriors, of course."

"Did President Grant weigh in on it?" Heck asked.

"Not that I know of. The report didn't mention him, even though he could've authorized it. The pundits think he's not gonna run for a third term, he's gonna follow in George Washington's footsteps. If you ask me, he's a died-in-the-wool soldier and not a politician, and he's tired of all the corruption that's been festering around him. The wheeler-dealers know how to take advantage of him. Hamilton Fish ain't gonna run neither. He's sixty-seven and he thinks he's too old."

"So, who's it gonna be?"

"If I had to guess, Hayes against Tilden, but don't take it to the bank. Washington's a crazy-ass place these days."

"Always has been," said Heck.

"Anyhow," said the sheriff, "I don't think Grant wants another uprising or another massacre on his watch, whites agin' Injuns. So, this Department of the Interior report shuffles the problem off to people like you and me, that way *their* asses are covered. It's up to us how we deal with this crazy medicine man and the shit falls on us if we make a mistake. Nocona's not just a thorn in our sides but a thorny cactus between our legs."

They chuckled sardonically.

"I'm pretty sure I know how the craziness got started," Heck said. "Some months ago, a few stray buffalo seemed to come out of nowhere and wandered onto the Sioux reservation, and the Injuns thought they must be ghosts of some of the lost herds. It was enough for Nocona to start start tellin' his followers that the herds were gonna come back."

"Yeah. I know. It ain't true no-how, but they wanna believe it. People believe what they wanna believe even if it don't make no sense. Take the Shoshones, for instance. Two of our Injun scouts said upwards of a thousand of 'em danced for three days and nights and they started writhin' on the ground like a bunch of Holy Rollers and shoutin' that Jesus was comin' back and was gonna make all us Whites die of some kinda disease and give the Injuns their land back. I know I'm kind of repeatin' what I was rantin' about earlier in my office, but I just can't believe what's happenin', Heck."

"I hear some of these Ghost Dancers take their clothes off and jump around with their dicks hangin' out," Heck said. "Can you imagine a thing like that, Dylan?"

"I don't even wanna think about it. You shouldn't of said it 'cause it's stuck in my mind now. My personal opinion is we pushed 'em too hard to give up all their traditions and makin' 'em cut their hair and wear our kinda clothes. They actually *hate* tryin' to be like us."

"I don't really blame 'em," Heck said. "But who or what is makin' 'em turn into cannibals?"

"I wish I knew. While you were gone, a rumor started up that Nocona is gonna lead another Ghost

Dance sometime in the next few days. That's what I got wind of. If my scouts can nail it down, you and Billy Hickok should go have a look-see. Not to cause trouble. Just to try and learn a bit more than we know right now."

"Makes sense," said Heck. "Long as we don't get ourselves scalped or skinned."

Dylan Parkman took a deep breath, then spoke in a lowered voice after looking around to make sure no one was eavesdropping. "One thing no one knows but me, Heck, and it can't go no further. Wild Bill ain't quite so wild no more because he's got vision problems."

"Yeah, when he's drunk, which is quite often," Heck said with a tight-lipped grin.

"No, I'm serious," said Parkman. "He just got back from seein' an eye specialist in Kansas City while he was there as part of Buffalo Bill's *Scouts of the Plains* exhibition. He had to quit the show because the bright lights affected his eyes."

Heck got serious and asked, "Did the specialist help him with that?"

"Naw, he doesn't even know what causes it. He told Billy that Jesse James hisself suffered from it, and it's common on the frontier. It's called opthalmia or a couple other things, but there's no cure. It might be from staring into hot, glaring sunshine so much of the time out here."

"Damn!" Heck said. "I wonder if I might be at risk from it."

"I hope not, but the worst part is, Billy has a lot of enemies who'd take a shot at him if they knew he can't see too good anymore."

"Then how's he gonna back me up if Nocona's Ghost Dancers attack us?" Heck said, staring at Dylan, challenging him for a good answer.

"Firing into a crowd comin' at you from a distance is no problem, is it? And when they're up close you and Billy both won't have no trouble drillin' 'em."

"Well, now, that just doesn't make me feel too damn comfortable, if you'll pardon me for saying so."

"Look here, Heck, Billy's a famous man down on his luck, and I don't wanna kick him while he's down. I give him stuff to do that takes him out of town for a while, so he won't get shot in the back sittin' at a poker table."

"That's right kind of you, Dylan, but like I said, it don't make me feel too goddamn comfortable."

CHAPTER 5

Heck Thomas, who was a steadfast lawman with a hard-won personal code of ethics, considered so-called "Wild Bill" Hickok to be a grandstander and a braggart. True enough, Bill was a skilled and deadly gunslinger and had even worked on the right side of the law much of his time on earth, but his flair for showmanship and manufactured notoriety made him untrustworthy, in Heck's opinion. At age thirty-nine, Wild Bill was already a hero of the dime novels. But his reputation wasn't totally unfounded. In real life he had been a soldier, scout, lawman, cattle rustler, gambler, stagecoach driver and showman.

He was tall and lean in buckskins trimmed with fringe and Indian-style beadwork, and he always wore two shiny long-barreled revolvers and a long-bladed Bowie knife on his belt. In the dime novels, he was portrayed with flowing brown hair, but in person his hair was flaming red. He also wore a red mustache, and Heck was once told by a saloon rowdy that back when he and Wild Bill used to be Kansas Jayhawkers, Billy was derisively known as "Duck Bill" because of his long nose and protruding lips, and had grown the mustache as a distraction.

In spite of the outlandish legends that had sprouted up around Wild Bill, some of his notable exploits had actually happened. He had once been mangled by a bear protecting her cubs and had managed to grab his knife and slit the she-bear's throat while she was on top of him. He could also transform himself into a gallant desperado when the occasion moved him. Suspected of shooting one particular outlaw while in concealment behind a curtain, the "unfairness" of it bothered him so much that he visited the dead man's widow and gave her all the money he had in his pocket -- thirty-nine dollars. He was rumored to have killed hundreds of men, but the true figure was about six, including Travis Trutt, whom he killed in a duel. Each man was allowed only one shot, and Trutt's shot missed Wild Bill, but Bill's shot slammed into Trutt's chest from seventy-five yards. The duel was fought over a gold watch that was lost by Bill in a poker game, but he maintained that Trutt was paid back in cash but was still keeping the watch. At trial, he was acquitted by a jury that ruled self-defense.

***

Two nights after Heck's discussion with Sheriff Dylan Parkman in the dining room of the Golden Nugget Hotel, Heck and Hickok sneaked up on two dozen or more Lakota Ghost Dancers by leaving their horses in a stand of trees, then crawling on their bellies under cover of darkness, till they got close enough to take a gander at the strange goings-on.

The writhing, shimmering dancers in dirty, ragged clothes seemed almost ghost-like in the dim, smoky glow of wooden stakes topped with flaming pitch. Their everyday garments, tattered and threadbare, were now worn underneath multi-colored shirts, gowns or serapes with faces or emblems of ancient gods and demons painted on them -- like the gruesome faces carved on totem poles.

Heck had to squint through the torch-lit semi-darkness to make out as many details as he could, which made him wonder how much Wild Bill could see, considering his vision problems.

The cult leader and medicine man, Nocona, sat cross-legged on the ground in the middle of the frenetic circle of dancers, smoking some kind of substance in a hand-carved ornamental pipe. The enraptured writhing and twisting, in rhythm to the pulse of a dozen drums, went on and on for the longest time, causing Wild Bill to murmur, "How much more of this shit do we have to watch?"

To which Heck said, "Shhh. Let's sneak back and get on our horses."

Billy realized Heck wasn't suggesting that they should haul ass out of there; they were just going to come back mounted and with their rifles.

CHAPTER 6

Nocona clapped his hands sharply and the ghost dance was brought to an abrupt end for the dancers who had a tough time coming out of their mind-blown trances.

Nocona rose to his feet and gazed into the distance upon hearing approaching hooves.

It was near dawn by now, and Heck Thomas and Wild Bill Hickok appeared seemingly out of nowhere and halted their horses just a few feet from the medicine man as he faced them with utter self-confidence and unwavering belief in himself and the prophesies he espoused. He was clad in a long buckskin coat painted with images of Lakota gods and devils. He also wore a broad red headband with no feathers stuck in it, but with the ends of it dangling behind his head.

Heck said, "You know who I am, Nocona, but you might not know Billy Hickok."

Nocona said, "I know he is feared. But I fear nobody."

Wild Bill said jeeringly, "Do tell, Mr. Nocona. Then you won't mind if we put a noose around your miserable neck that'll look nice with your featherless headband."

Nocona stood still and stolid, with nary a murmur.

Heck decided to try to rattle him. He said, "The Brewster family, sheep ranchers down the road from here, were massacred by some kind of miscreants that like to eat human flesh. Cannibals used to stay where they belong, but now they seem to be among us for some reason."

Nocona said, "And where do they belong, according to you, Mr. Thomas?"

"In the jungles in South America or Africa. Up till now I never heard of such a thing in any part of this continent. Did you?"

"I know nothing of such things."

"Well, I suspect that you do. I think some of your so-called Ghost Dancers must've gone off the deep end. They follow your teachings, so that makes you just as guilty. I also think you must know who or what these fucking cannibals are."

Nocona flashed a tight, grim smile. He said, "I can assure you that my teachings are nonviolent. My disciples wear shirts that can stop arrows and bullets. They dance to bring forth a new world which will be ushered in by floods, tornadoes, landslides and earthquakes. The earth will be rolled up like a carpet with all the white man's ugly things wrapped inside -- sheep, pigs, fences, telegraph poles, trains and stagecoaches. The whites will disappear, rolled up in

27

the Great Spirit's majestic carpet. Our dead will come back to us, as will the herds of buffalo the whites have slaughtered.

"Poppycock!" Wild Bill savagely blurted.

Nocona eyed him with unmitigated and deep-seated contempt. He said, "I sense that you were one of those buffalo killers. Not hunters. Just killers. You shot the innocent beasts from railroad cars while you drank brandy and smoked fat black machine-rolled cigars. You left thousands of our sacred animals rotting on the prairie."

"Soon's as I git a chance I'll shoot *you* and leave *you* to rot, too!" Wild Bill jeered.

"The Great Spirit will protect me."

"How's about we take a chance and see. Are you up for it?"

"I do not play games with the Great Spirit's omens."

"So go fuck yourself," said Wild Bill.

CHAPTER 7

Two gravediggers, Bart Crasten and Larry Wallace, were almost finished making four individual graves for the dead members of the Brewster family. They had already set wooden crosses over two of the graves, those of the mother and the father, and were hammering crosses into the earth at the heads of the smaller graves where Letty and her brother now resided.

They stood back and Bart said, "Lord knows, I ain't no preacher, but I figure we oughta say somethin' proper."

Larry said, "How's about the Lord's Prayer?"

"Okay, I guess, but I might not remember all the words, so let's say it together."

"Let's take our hats off, and let's just say somethin' short."

Larry and Bart had been enlisted to come out here by Sheriff Dylan Parkman. He had found them in one of the crummiest saloons in Deadwood, as usual, and that's where he had shown them a pick and two shovels lying in the bed of a mule-drawn cart, along with enough wooden planks to make the crosses. Then he had sternly told them, "You better do a good job and don't just sell the tools I've given you and get yourselves drunk, 'cause I'll hunt your sorry asses down and put you in the clink for a year or more on bread and water. On the other hand, you come back here and swear you done it right, I'll give each of you three dollars."

"How's about five?" Larry had dared to ask.

And the sheriff had said, "Nope. Three."

Thirteen years ago, Bart and Larry had been conscripted to serve in the Confederate army, but had deserted as soon as they got a chance, and had never tried to amount to much thereafter. Now, today, they both felt they had been conscripted to be grave diggers.

"But at least we're gettin' paid," Bart said.

"And we don't have to be in a fuckin' uniform," Larry added.

They both wore torn and faded flannel shirts, old hats with the crowns crushed and battered, and filthy wool trousers with ropes through the loops instead of belts. Their beards were wild and scraggly, and their hobnail boots were cracked and mud-caked. Yet they were hard workers for short stretches, and when they actually managed to finish a piece of work, they took pride in it.

"I ain't much for fancy words," Bart said. "You got somethin' in mind, you say it."

They doffed their beat-up hats and got somber looks on their faces as they stood over the four graves.

"Ashes to ashes, dust to dust," Larry said. "And may perpetual light shine upon them."

"Amen," Bart said. "There. It's done. I'm dry, but I wanna save the water that's still left in my canteen. I'm gonna go in the house and look for some hard cider or somethin'. Might get lucky and find some."

"Maybe even moonshine," Larry said, brightening. "You go ahead. I'll put the tools in the wagon."

The mule-drawn cart furnished by the sheriff was parked a short distance from the fresh graves, and Larry picked up the tools and headed that way.

Bart meandered toward the sod house, which had no door, just a coarse blanket hung over the entrance. He pulled the covering aside and went in.

He found the inside dimly lit, thanks to four crude windows in the sod walls. None of the windows had glass in them; they were just rectangular holes.

Bart blinked his eyes, trying to get accustomed to the dim light -- when suddenly he was pounced upon by a Lakota warrior wearing a Ghost Shirt!

The ferocity of the attack knocked Bart down onto the dirt floor, with the dead-looking warrior clawing and biting at his face and throat. Bart tried to fight back -- but then a second being joined in, biting and clawing.

Larry, who was waiting by the mule-drawn cart for Bart to reappear, took a swig from his canteen, then bit off a chew from a chunk of tobacco wrapped in wax paper. Thinking that Bart may have found some liquor and was polishing it off by his lonesome, he headed toward the sod house and stepped inside -- but he didn't get far. The two ferocious beings, scowling and rasping, jumped on Larry and pushed him down, and he kicked and flailed as they started biting into him.

The last thing he saw before he became undead was his buddy Bart kneeling down and biting a big chunk of flesh from his soft throat.

CHAPTER 8

Nocona was locked in a cell and Sheriff Parkman was staring at him through the bars.

"How's it feel?" the sheriff asked him, with a sneer on his face, because Nocona had been stripped of his long leather Ghost Dance coat after Heck and Billy arrested him, stripped him down to his breechclout and brought him in, tied down onto a travois, the way the Lakota dragged their rolled-up teepees from camp to camp.

Heck had explained, "We didn't have no other way of gettin' him here. Only reason his followers stood still for it was 'cause he ordered them to. He used Jesus's own words from the Bible. Them that lives by the sword will die by the sword. You believe he said them kinda things, Dylan?"

"I'll damn near believe anything these days," the sheriff had said. "What's up is down and down is up."

Now, facing Nocona in his cell, Sheriff Parkman informed him that he was going to have a visitor.

"I won't speak with any visitors," Nocona said stubbornly.

"You won't have to say nothin' you don't wanna say," said the sheriff. "My hangman wants to see you to size you up for a noose and a drop so the rope don't tear your head off and don't strangle you slowly 'stead of breakin' your neck good and proper. His name is George Maledon. He tells funny stories while he's sizin' people up. You'll enjoy his company so much you'll forget what he's here for."

Nocona said, "I don't need any stupid white men's fables. I don't believe in your Christian Bible, which was crammed down my throat thirty or forty times a day at the Indian School in Carlisle. I'm surprised they didn't try to bleach my skin white. I had to pretend to believe in their prayers so I wouldn't get beaten or sexually abused. When I become lonely, I speak with my revered ancestors. They are my spiritual guardians."

Sheriff Parkman snorted derisively because he was a Methodist through and through, but beneath his derision he actually felt empathy for Nocona; the same empathy he would feel for any human being made to suffer from cruelty. Still, he had to defend his faith, so he said, "You might see your ancestors in your dreams or up in the clouds, but they sure ain't down here walkin' around no more." His secret truth was that he had a hard time believing that his own dead loved ones were gallivanting up in the clouds, too.

Nocona said, defiantly, "You are a nonbeliever, but you will soon regret your ignorant ways, white man."

Taking refuge in his own brand of defiance, Dylan Parkman said, "Maybe I'll go to hell for some of the things I've done, but between then and now, I'm gonna get to see you hang. And I'm gonna celebrate by gettin' sloppy drunk with my buddies, Heck Thomas and Wild Bill and George Maledon hisself. A New York publisher put out a comic book about George that was mostly bullshit -- they called him the Prince of Hangmen -- so you should be honored to meet him."

"You'll be watching the wrong man dangling at the end of a rope if you do that to me, Sheriff Parkman. I had nothing to do with what happened to the Brewster family. But I know who did."

"Humph! Don't try to push it off onto someone else just to save your own hide. You're the one who's got those damned Ghost Dancers all riled up, and don't try to tell me otherwise."

Nocona said, "I preach love and kindness, but my brother preaches rape, vengeance and murder."

Taken aback, Sheriff Parkman said, "You say you have a brother? Then why didn't I ever hear about him?"

"He has been in Mexico leading a band of Comancheros, whites who rape and pillage in the guise of Apaches. He is my evil twin. He came out of my mother's womb right after I did, and, according to our beliefs, she should have smothered him. But instead, she hid him in some bushes and he was saved

35

by a white farm woman. A witch. In our culture, giving birth to twins or triplets is taboo. Only the lower animals have litters, and if two or more babies are born together, one of them must be good and one must be evil, like my twin brother. His name is Otarro, and he vows to destroy me. Your white preachers would call him a minion of Satan. But we of the Lakota Nation do not believe in your gods or your devils."

Even as Nocona spoke those words, his twin brother was taking advantage of the absence of a strong leader of the Ghost Dancers to launch a surprise attack against them. Nocona himself did not know that Notarro's band of ruthless Comancheros had fled Mexico, chased over the border by *Federales* determined to wipe them out, in the same way that their counterparts of thirty years ago had wiped out the defenders of The Alamo.

It was twilight in the Lakota encampment, and about two dozen Ghost Dancers were dancing in a large circle, round and round, chanting and writhing in the way Nocona had taught them, as he himself had been taught in visions from the Lakota gods. The drums were beating and the torches were flaming as the dance went on and on in a clearing surrounded by tied-up dogs, horses and cattle, and by the teepees of the Lakota people.

Pounding hooves and war cries began to intrude from some distance beyond the wide circle of frenetic dancers. When they realized what they were hearing, they started to run and scatter. But too late.

Ten to fifteen whooping, screaming, half-naked bareback riders started blasting away at the fleeing Ghost Dancers, none of whom were armed at the beginning of the attack -- but even so, four or five of them succeeded in dragging one of the attackers down off of his horse and they pounded his head and body with rocks until they were shot full of arrows and bullet holes.

With over a dozen Ghost Dancers' bodies scattered over the very ground they were dancing on, their attackers kept whooping and screaming their battle cries and shooting more bullets and arrows into them -- as their leader, Otarro -- with his black hair in braids and his bare chest, arms and legs covered with evil-looking tattoos -- rode in their midst, wheeling his painted pony in circles and shouting:

"Mutilate them! Stab their eyes out! Bite into their flesh! Scalp them! Make their bodies so ugly that the Great Spirit will shun them! Make their souls wander forever in the Land of the Undead!"

CHAPTER 9

Unaware that a massacre had taken place the previous night, Jed Harris, a telegraph company lineman, shimmied up a pole in the hot sun, where a line of wooden poles stretched to the horizon. Jed was wearing hobnail boots and using a harness for safety. His wide leather belt supported a leather pouch full of tools, and he was wearing a flannel shirt, blue jeans, and a cap with the logo of the Deadwood Telegraph Company. A horse-drawn wagon bearing the same logo was parked in the shade of a nearby tree, and Jed's dog, Barney, was asleep in the bed of the wagon.

After making his climb up to the high wires, Jed found a wire that was cut into as if with a knife, and he shook his head, muttering to himself.

"Damn savages don't understand dots and dashes. They think we're supposed to use smoke signals."

He set to work with wire cutters, pliers and splicing tape.

Meantime, three shambling, scowling, dead-looking entities emerged from the woods and approached his wagon. Jed didn't know it, but they actually *were* dead! They were three of the Ghost

Dancers slaughtered and mutilated by Otarro and his band of Comancheros, and their wounds were truly ghastly. Their dead faces stared up at Jed, drooling, showing their hunger for live human flesh.

High up as he was, Jed failed to hear their approach and was unaware of their presence.

But Barney's ears pricked up, and he awakened when he smelled the approaching ghouls. He started barking and straining at the leash that kept him from jumping out of the wagon.

Startled by all the commotion, Jed started shimmying down the pole.

The zombies' hands were reaching for the dog, clawing at him and choking him.

Barney bit into a ghoulish hand, snarling viciously and hanging on. Both Barney and the ghoul tumbled to the ground.

"Barney!" Jed yelled in panic.

One of the ghouls smashed a rock at Barney's head, and the dog howled. The ghoul smashed him with the rock again and again.

With his head a bloody mess, Barney whimpered and died.

Jed jumped down from the pole now, his harness strap dangling from his waist. He pulled the best weapons he had -- a big screwdriver and a claw hammer -- from his leather tool pouch.

Consumed with rage over the death of Barney, Jed advanced upon the three flesh-hungry zombies. He tried to bash one of them in the head with his hammer, but he missed, dealing only a glancing blow to the dead creature's shoulder. The other two started to close in on him and he felt like a calf being harassed and sniped at, circled by coyotes.

He jabbed his long-bladed screwdriver at one of the zombies' eyes, and that zombie backed away, but the other two kept drooling and slavering, unfazed.

Jed came at them, swinging his hammer and jabbing with his screwdriver. But the third one tackled him by his legs. He fell, dropping his screwdriver but managing to hang onto his hammer.

He thrashed and struggled, trying to get back up, but the zombie who tackled him was lying across his legs. With great effort he started to crawl away, dragging the zombie who was now clutching him by his ankles.

Finally Jed got halfway up and smashed his hammer down on top of the clutching zombie's head. He smashed again and again, and that zombie was done for, its yellowish dead eyes staring straight up into the sky, its cracked head oozing dark blood.

Jed looked up to see five more zombies coming at him from the edge of the woods. Like the other three, they were wearing the usual Lakota clothes, but some had long shirts or gowns covered with painted symbols.

Jed scrambled to his feet and ran, with the zombies in slow, shambling pursuit. Then, three more zombies emerged from yet another wooded path, blocking his escape.

He stopped in his tracks, still wielding his hammer but not knowing if it will do him much good.

Suddenly, he heard galloping hooves -- and a huge palomino horse charged three of the menacing ghouls.

Jed saw, to his amazement, that the rider was a young woman, her pretty face locked in determination, her long blonde hair streaming behind her as she aimed a lever-action rifle and immediately fired it, hitting one of the zombies in its head.

She wheeled her palomino in the nick of time, facing two zombies who were about to claw at her and shooting both of them up close. Two head shots brought them down.

But the others started closing on her.

She yelled, "Quick! Get on!"

Jed barely hesitated. He jumped onto the palomino, behind its rider, and grabbed her by her hips as she dug her spurs in and they hit a fast gallop, narrowly getting away from the advancing ghouls.

CHAPTER 10

St. Willard's Catholic Church and School, nestled in a clearing in the woods, about twenty miles from Deadwood, was surrounded by more than a dozen ghouls. Some were Whites, some were Indians, some were male, some were female, before they became *undead*. Some were wearing only breechclouts, some were in bibbed coveralls, and some wore neckerchiefs and chaps. Some were housewives in cheap dresses, but of course had become somehow transformed. All of them were ghouls, hungrily salivating, terrifyingly anxious to get inside and devour the living.

The church was not a hulking, virtually impregnable stone structure with stained glass windows. It was a modest little wood-frame building serving poor settlers and country folk. Its windows were tall and narrow, of ordinary glass. Most of the windows were boarded up, but even so some of them had been shattered by the zombies outside.

The school consisted of one plain room with twenty desks for kids of various ages. In a corner was a little desk with a telegraph set. A short hallway led into a church so small it could be more appropriately called a chapel, but it had a potbellied stove, a modest altar, crude charcoal drawings of the Stations of the Cross posted on the two longest walls, and a short row of pews for Sunday attendance.

Trapped and surrounded by what to them felt like an army of ghouls, were Father Ed, the pastor of what, to him, was a religious oasis in the middle of nowhere; and Sister Hillary, a kindly and resourceful nun who wore a nun's habit, but was not shrouded in black from head to toe. Instead, she was clad in a prim white blouse and a black skirt that came down past her knees.

Notable among the other scared people looking to the priest and the nun for protection and guidance were:

Annie Kimball, a bright, winsome twelve-year-old, the oldest of the children being taught at St. Willard's, thus relied on by Sister Hillary to help out with classroom chores, including tutoring some of the younger kids.

Janice Kimball, Annie's fussy, bespectacled mother, who works as a volunteer Teacher's aide.

Pete Gilley, a forty-five-year-old janitor and caretaker, in clodhoppers and bibbed coveralls. Buck-toothed and not very bright, he was a cigar smoker with a drinking problem.

Bertie Samuels, a spoiled, pampered nine-year-old who can't control himself because he's so frightened.

All of them are hoping to be somehow rescued.

43

The boards over the smashed windows mostly came from broken-up school desks and benches, but Father Ed was still trying to make the place more secure. In his hands he had a hammer and nails, and was trying to hold a chunk of desk in place and pound a nail into it at the same time. He turned and called out, "Annie, will you give me a hand, please!"

Annie jumped up and held the board in place while Father Ed drove his nails. He pulled on the board to assess whether it could stop ghouls from getting it, and he wasn't sure, but it would have to do.

He smiled at Annie and said, "Thanks, honey."

She was one of the school's brightest children, also cute without hardly trying. She had short reddish hair, blue eyes and freckles, and she was wearing a calico dress made by her mom.

"Nice work, Annie!" Sister Hillary called out from just inside the doorway to the church. Then she turned to a group of frightened young children who were clustered close to one another, sitting on desks that hadn't been destroyed to make window barriers. "You see, children, we're doing the right thing," she told them encouragingly. "We'll be safe here, and all our prayers will be answered. The sheriff will bring a posse as soon as our telegraph is working again. We must trust in Almighty God."

But the spoiled kid, Bertie Samuels, wasn't reassured one bit, and he started wailing.

"We're doomed, Sister Hillary! We're *doomed!* No one knows we're here all by ourselves! We're surrounded! There won't be any posse! I want my daddy!"

Mustering as much calmness as she could, Sister Hillary said, "You'll be seeing your father soon enough, Bertie. He can't come to you right now. It's too dangerous out there."

Bertie wailed louder. "I want my *daddy!"*

"Shush!" Father Ed hoarsely whispered. "They can hear you. You might make them move in closer."

Annie Kimball and her mother, Janice, had moved to another window, on the opposite side of the room, and they saw the zombies doing exactly what Father Ed feared. They were moving in closer, milling around, seemingly more alert than before, sniffing for the scent of fresh human flesh.

Annie gasped. "Oh, my God, Mom! There are more of them! Look!"

Janice spun around, facing the others in the room and saying, "She's right! We'll never get out of here alive!" She made the Sign of the Cross over herself.

The kids shuddered and some of them started to cry.

Little Bertie cried hardest.

Father Ed faced Janice and said, "Calm down, Janice, please. You're scaring the kids worse."

Janice grimaced and pursed her lips. She told Father Ed, "When I volunteered to become a teacher's aide, I don't remember this kind of thing being in the church bulletin."

Father Ed said, "I'm glad you can at least joke about it."

And she snapped, "I wasn't joking!"

She rejoined Annie at the window and immediately turned away, looking stunned. "Now there really are *more* of them!" she blurted. "Where can they all be coming from?"

Sister Hillary said, "Come, children, come with me. Let's go into the church. Help me lead them in prayer, Janice."

"Forgive me, Sister," Janice said, "but I wonder if prayer is going to help us. Maybe this is God's punishment for our sins."

Father Ed cut in a bit chidingly. "Don't blaspheme, Janice. We teach the faithful that prayer always helps. Every prayer is answered, in the Lord's good time and in His own way. God always listens."

Bertie wailed louder than ever. He cried out, "Even if a posse comes we're all gonna be found dead! I want my daddy...I want my daddy...I want my daddy..."

CHAPTER 11

After they were pretty sure they were a goodly distance from the ghouls who were pursuing them, Danielle slowed her horse to a trot. She and Jed were both rattled and breathing hard, but he managed to say, "Thanks. You saved my life. What is your name?"

"Danielle," she told him without glancing back over her shoulder.

They rode on, and he was sort of embarrassed to have his hands on her hips. He had always been shy around women and had envied the guys who weren't. Having seen Danielle in action under dire circumstances, he already realized how courageous she was, in addition to being pretty, and this made him even less capable of submerging his shyness.

Lamely, he said, "I'm sorry, Danielle, I didn't mean to put you in danger."

"You didn't," she said. "None of it was your fault. But what are you doing out here without a gun? Don't you know what's happening?"

He was trying to come up with an answer, but the palomino took them around a bend and they could see the Brewsters' sod house in the distance. When they got closer they saw the four recent graves, and they both dismounted.

"This is where you were headed all along?" Jed asked her.

She barely listened to him. Instead, she headed straight toward the four graves. But she stopped short and started crying and trembling.

Standing slightly behind her, Jed reached as if to put his arm around her, then decided against it.

Still shedding tears, she spoke in a near whisper.

"It's true...it's true...just like Billy Hickok said. He said two gravediggers were sent here by Sheriff Parkman, but neither one ever came back. They were probably attacked too, and carried off to God only knows where."

Bewildered, he said, "I don't know why, but I got attacked, too. Who *are* they? They killed my dog...they must be sick...like mad dogs..."

"They're not crazy -- they're *dead!*" Danielle blurted angrily.

"That's impossible!"

"Well, that's what everyone thought -- up until yesterday. Wild Bill spilled the beans while he was drunk as a hoot-owl in my daddy's saloon. I was waiting on tables. I heard him babbling about Heck Thomas finding the Brewster family cannibalized. Dave and Mary are my aunt and uncle and their two kids are my cousins. Or were. I was headed here but I got sidetracked when I spotted you in big trouble."

Jed told her, "I found a break in the telegraph line and was about to fix it. I left my gun and holster in the wagon when I had to put on my tool belt. I never minded being out here in the boondocks on my own. I enjoy the freedom from civilization. Just me and my dog, Barney. But now...now Barney is dead."

"What's your name?"

"Jed Harris."

"Well, I'm Danielle, like I told you. Danielle Greer. I work in my daddy's saloon. I don't let none of the roughnecks get fresh with me neither, and they damn well know not to try it."

Jed's shyness came rushing back because he took what she was saying as a warning. He said, "We figured a telegraph line must be down since the pastor of St. Willard's church, a few miles from here, checks in with us every day, but two days went by without him getting in touch. It's not only a church but a one-room school, so Father Ed has his own telegraph system in case of any kind of emergency."

"He knows how to operate it?"

"He was a communications officer in the Civil War. He's not just some namby-pamby fellow in a clerical collar running around with a Bible in his hand."

"I hate to tell you this," Danielle said, "but we had better check out the school. By now they could be surrounded."

"Surrounded by what? What would you call them? Nut cases? Mentally diseased?"

"I don't know *what* to call them, except *ghouls*. Right now there's a Lakota medicine man in the town jail, and he's been claiming that his dead ancestors are coming back to life. He doesn't call them ghouls or cannibals, he calls them Skin Dancers. *Whatever* they are, they have to be killed. It's us or them."

CHAPTER 12

A piano player wearing a bowler hat with a red hatband, a crisp white shirt with red and blue stripes, and a red-and-white bowtie, was loudly playing and singing '*Oh, Susanna*' in Jesse Greer's Union Saloon. Jesse was Danielle Greer's father, and he had named the place as a declaration of his sympathies with the troops in blue who had fought against the Confederacy about a decade ago, and were fighting against Indians now.

Jesse was sitting with a group of high-rolling poker players and smoking a fat cigar, enjoying the rise and fall of the players' fortunes, and loving the house percentage being raked in out of each big pot.

He looked to his left as Sheriff Parkman barged through the swinging doors and headed his way, his sharp gray eyes taking in the table top piled with stacks of poker chips, beer and shot glasses, and bottles of whiskey. Wild Bill Hickok was playing poker with Heck Thomas and two smoothly handsome and well-dressed fellows wearing string ties, white shirts and pinstripe suits with black vests.

"Howdy, Sheriff," Jesse Greer said.

Wild Bill said, "Wanna sit in, Dylan? Meet Wyatt Earp and John Holliday, known as Doc Holliday. They come here by stagecoach last night from Tombstone."

Wyatt said, "Pleased to meet you, Sheriff."

Doc Holliday said, "Likewise."

Sheriff Parkman said, "Well, you two gentleman must know your reputations precede you."

Wyatt said, "Much exaggerated, I'm afraid. We're harmless unless riled."

The other card players chuckled knowingly.

Sheriff Parkman wasn't kidding about Wyatt Earp's reputation preceding him. All lawmen in the Territories knew Earp had to be watched closely should he show up in their towns, most of which already had more than their share of ruffians.

Just four years earlier, in Peoria, Illinois, Earp was arrested aboard a fifty-foot keelboat, the *Beardstown*, which was outfitted with a ramshackle eight-bedroom house, used as a floating brothel. To evade local authorities, the boat would dock and pick up horny passengers, then make slow trips down the Illinois River, tying up at points along the way. Along with Earp, who had previously been arrested and fined for pimping in other Western towns, the owner of the establishment, John Walton, was handcuffed and jailed, and so was a sixteen-year-old prostitute, plus eight older women practicing the sex trade.

The *Peoria Daily Democrat* classified Wyatt Earp as "a contemptible loafer, a beggar, a man of poor character, a tramp and a pimp." But Earp and Walton were not jailed for long; instead they were each fined forty-four dollars and sent on their way "to do their dirty work elsewhere," according to the newspaper.

Be that as it may, Sheriff Parkman had to take sort of a "charitable view" of unsavory characters like Earp, otherwise he'd need to arrest half the men in Deadwood. Many of them started out wild and reckless, but end up honorable, or even noteworthy.

After the sheriff sat at the gambling table, Jesse Greer said, "I'm going to welcome some customers who just came in. One of them's a judge. Don't talk too loud about stuff you might not want him to hear." He got up and headed toward the bar.

Sheriff Parkman took the vacated chair and sat in it, scooting it closer to the table. He said, "Deal me in, Mr. Earp. I don't think I could beat your *fast* draw, but perhaps I can beat you at five-*card* draw."

"This is a high-stakes game," Doc Holliday informed him. "If it's too rich for you, we can lower the ante for a hand or two."

"No, let's keep it high," said the sheriff. "I had some luck yesterday, so I'm heeled and I maybe can keep my streak goin'."

"I sincerely hope not," said the dapper Doc Holliday, with a polite and gentlemanly grin.

Wyatt Earp said to Sheriff Parkman, "My friend the doc is rumored to have killed a couple dozen men, but truly he's only done two or three in self-defense or in duels that are legal down South, where he's from. He's got a degree in dentistry from a college in Philadelphia."

"I plan to practice here in Deadwood for at least a while," said Doc Holliday. "Out of my rooms at the Golden Nugget Hotel. I have won awards for the Best Set of Teeth in Gold, and also the Best Set of Teeth in Vulcanized Rubber."

"Yep, I saw that in your ad in the *Deadwood News Picayune*, but I still got my own teeth so far," Sheriff Parkman said.

"I'd much rather help folks than shoot them," the doc said. "I'm no trouble most of the time, and I don't go looking for it."

"I can imagine that your reputation, whether it's real or exaggerated, has a tendency to draw trouble to ya," the sheriff acknowledged.

"Well, you've got that right. Unfortunately," Doc Holliday said in his soft Georgia drawl.

The sheriff noted that he had a boyish face and with his blue eyes and neatly barbered ash-blonde hair, he looked too young to be either a dentist or a gunslinger. So maybe it was true that he wasn't by nature a troublemaker. But trouble seemed to follow him, so the sheriff decided to keep a close watch on him.

CHAPTER 13

Nine-year-old Bertie Samuels was curled up in a ball, lying on the schoolhouse floor, wailing and wailing over and over about how badly he wanted his daddy.

Pete Gilley, the janitor, came into the room carrying a toolbox. He eyed Bertie with a grimace of distaste, then put his toolbox down with a thud on top of one of the intact school desks. He said, "I can't take that brat any more. I gotta get outta here."

Janice Kimball said, "He can't help it. He's just a little kid, and he's scared."

As usual, Sister Hillary annoyed Pete by quoting the Bible. "Suffer the little children to come unto me. That's what Jesus would've told you, Pete."

"Yeah, well, the brat's makin' *me* suffer. What about that, huh?"

Janice looked up after peering into the potbellied stove. "The fire's gone out. I'm cold. Don't we have any more logs, Pete?"

Pete sneered at her, then went to a boarded-up window and squinted between the nailed-up boards.

Behind his back, Janice put her index finger to her temple and made little circles with it.

Pete turned from the window and almost caught her at it. With heavy sarcasm, he said to her, "We got plenty of logs if you wanna go out and get 'em. I bet you don't. Mebbe them things out there will be more'n glad to carry an armload in for ya. I see three of 'em standin' by the log pile with helpful looks on their faces."

Pete turned from the window and looked all around the room to make sure no one was paying much attention to him. Then he sneaked off to a cupboard that held cleaning supplies. He slowly opened the cupboard door so as not to make any noise, then rummaged behind some stacked-up soap bars and pulled out a half-pint flask of whiskey and furtively uncapped it. He chugged down a couple of gulps. Then he wiped his mouth and slipped the flask into a side pocket of his coveralls.

He went to his toolbox, still on top of one of the kids' desks, took out a sharp chisel, and tucked it into one of his back pockets. To anyone who might be watching him, he piped up.

"Wish I had a shotgun, but all I got is a box of tools. I had a beautiful Colt Peacemaker, but I lost it in a poker game. I guess mebbe one of them critters might back off if I was to stab his eye out with this chisel. I don't know why I should stay here. I got my horse, Lightning, tied up beside the shed, and them cannibals ain't comin' after *him* -- I guess they only like human meat, not horsemeat, but I wish it was t'other way around. I 'member when Gen'ral Crook's cavalry had to eat horsemeat, but they sure didn't enjoy it. God h'ep me if I had to butcher my own horse like they did. Lightning ain't really lightning fast, but he's fast enough. If I could get to him, I could make a break for it, and we'd both be long gone from this scary situation. I think we can do it. Them dead critters is slow-moving, like as if they got some rigor-mortis in 'em."

Father Ed had come through the hallway that led to the church, so he had heard the last part of Pete's ramble. "There are too many of them," he said to Pete. "And they stink! Your horse might rear up and drop you like a sack of manure."

"You're callin' me a sack of shit?" Pete said indignantly. "I thought priests wasn't s'posed to talk like that."

"I was just trying to shake you up so you'd stop letting foolish ideas creep into your head. If you go out there you won't last long, Pete."

"That's what you think, Father Ed. Lightning could zigzag right through 'em, or even trample a few of 'em like when I was a courier for Gen'ral Crook and had to creep through Grant's Union lines."

"I hate to say it, Pete, but you don't have those kinds of skills anymore, let alone sharp eyesight. Stay with us and wait it out."

"Goddamn it!" Pete snapped. "Don't you see? There's more and more of 'em out there. They're liable to break in at any time. This piss-ant place don't even have a basement for us to hide in. One of your puny barricades gives way, we're all gonna be zombie feed."

Defiantly, he took out his flask and gulped down a slug. The he grabbed a stove match and lit a cigar stub from his bib pocket, sucked in a lung full of smoke, and blew it out in rings.

Father Ed eyed him in disapproval, but said nothing.

But Sister Hillary couldn't take it. She said, "Pete! Shame on you! Drinking and smoking not twenty feet from the chapel. And swearing, too -- in front of the children!"

"I'm sick and tired of your rules, Sister! If I have to die, I'm goin' out drinkin' and smokin' and not havin' a nicotine fit."

He jammed the cigar butt between his lips, inhaled mightily, and blew out another chorus of smoke rings.

Two six-year-old boys giggled. They were both in short pants and short-sleeved shirts with neat little neckties.

Father Ed eyed Pete angrily and said, "Put that cigar out right now, or I'll fire you."

"You don't have to fire me, I quit! I'm gettin' outta here. Don't try to stop me!"

Father Ed considered his options, then gave up. Sadly he said, "I'll follow you to the back door and make sure it's locked after you go out. And may the Lord have mercy on your soul."

Pete said almost pleadingly, "You sure you don't have at least a rusty old shotgun somewhere around this place?"

"Jesus said those who live by the sword shall die by the sword. I'm sure he would've said the same thing about guns."

"But the Bible also says there's a time for all things, Father, and it's time for me to get the hell outta here."

CHAPTER 14

An attractive woman about thirty years old held the reins of a horse-drawn buckboard as it bounced over the ruts in the hard-packed mud of Deadwood's main street. She wore a long black dress and had her long dark hair tied into a bun, and there was a serious, no-nonsense air about her.

She pulled up in front of the Union Saloon and, gathering her skirts around her, she jumped down from the buckboard and went in through the swinging doors.

Her name was Martha Jane Canary, otherwise known as Calamity Jane, and when she was on a mission, nobody dared mess with her. She was known for wearing the same garments as men on the frontier, in other words leathers and buckskins, but underneath all that she was pretty and distinctly feminine.

She was born in 1852 in Princeton, Missouri, and took pride in that both Jesse and Frank James were born there. Tales of their exploits and derring-do fired her imagination as she was growing up. For her, it was a dream come true when her mom and pop decided to head West with her and her five siblings by wagon train. But along the way, both her parents died of pneumonia, and she, as the eldest, had to start taking care of the siblings on her own. She worked as a dishwasher, cook, waitress, dance hall girl, nurse, and ox team driver, and then as a scout in Wyoming Territory, and as such, was involved in some of the ongoing battles, cavalry against Indians.

During a skirmish in 1873 on Goose Creek, six of her fellow soldiers were killed, and she was wounded in an ambush. Although a bullet pierced her shoulder, she managed to pull her badly wounded captain from his saddle to hers, and rode with his bleeding body in front of her all the way back to their camp, where army surgeons pulled him through.

She came to Deadwood in the early part of 1876 in a wagon train led by Billy Hickok, and that's who she had come to see, all prettied up, in her favorite black dress.

Casting a sharp-eyed glance all around the raucous smoke-filled saloon, she fastened on the table with the poker players and headed straight over there, stopping abruptly a few feet away as Wild Bill immediately noticed her and smiled.

The other card players, Heck Thomas, Sheriff Parkman, Wyatt Earp and Doc Holiday, eyed her appreciatively, but held their silence, finding her attractive in a stern but still ladylike way.

Wild Bill said, "My, my, look at you, Jane! You sure get my britches hot when you're all dolled up."

She said, "Shush up, Bill. I need money for groceries and a couple bottles of good red wine. I'm grilling steaks for dinner. I was hoping you'd have a pile of chips in front of you and I'd get here before you blew it all."

Hickok said, "Sure, honey, and after we eat and drink, promise me you'll let me take my time unlacing that purty dress and the petticoats and lacey stuff underneath. You know that's my favorite thing, babe."

Coyly, Calamity Jane said, "Well...maybe. You treat me nice and I'll treat you nicer."

All this time the poker players had been sitting there with freshly dealt hands they hadn't bet on yet.

Hickok said, "Not to delay our little game a bit longer, gentlemen, but you're lookin' at my lovely wife -- my little canary. That's the name I tease her with but she doesn't like it. She's Martha Jane Canary -- pronounced *Cannery* -- known by most folks as Calamity Jane."

Calamity said, "I don't like to be called a canary because that's a stool pigeon, and I ain't no such thing. I appreciate it when I get a compliment or two when I'm all dressed up, but I can dress purty and I can dress rough, depending on what I'm up to at the moment. When I was a cavalry scout, I wore leathers and I could fight as hard as any of the men. You could ask some of the Injuns I went after, except none of them lived to tell the tale."

Wyatt Earp looked at Calamity Jane, leaned back and flashed a handsome smile.

Doc Holliday said, "I'm pleased to tell you that is one of the most charming introductions of a female person that I ever heard."

"Billy, you're a lucky man to have such a wife," said Heck Thomas.

CHAPTER 15

The back door of the school house creaked as it came open slightly. Garbage cans were stacked beside it on a slab of concrete.

The door creaked again as Father Ed and Pete Gilley peeked out. They scoped out the shed, made of split logs with a tin roof that stood at the edge of the clearing. It appeared that no zombies were close by.

Pete took a big slug of whiskey, then tucked his flask back in his coveralls.

Father Ed said, "Good luck, Pete. I wish you'd change your mind."

In dead seriousness, Pete said, "You all are at their mercy in here, Father. I advise you to make a break for it same as I'm tryin' to do. Some of you might die, but some of you might get away."

"We all have to make our choices," Father Ed said. "I believe the good Lord will protect us. After all, we're in God's house."

"Then why does God even let this evil exist? If there is a God, which I doubt."

Father Ed blessed himself with the Sign of the Cross, then said, "May the Lord forgive and protect you, Pete."

"I know you mean well, Father, but I ain't countin' on it.

He went out and Father Ed closed the door.

Pete took his chisel out of his back pocket, held it in front of him, and crept stealthily across the backyard toward the shed -- and to his surprise he not only got there safely but saw his horse, Lightning, still tied up there.

Three zombies noticed him and started to drool.

He hurriedly seized Lightning's reins.

The zombies came closer.

He slid his right foot into a stirrup -- but then an undead creature lurched at him from the other side of the shed, got him in a bear hug and made him drop his chisel.

Pete and the zombie both fell -- but Pete scrambled for the chisel when he saw it gleaming in the moonlight, not far from his hand.

He tightened his fist around it and plunged it into one of the zombie's eye sockets.

The zombie screamed -- a hideous unearthly sound -- and tried to pull the chisel out, but couldn't do it. He reeled and fell and lay still.

By now, two other zombies were clawing at Pete, pushing him to the ground again. He struggled mightily, but they kept biting and clawing even more ferociously.

A third zombie plunged a dead claw-like hand into Pete's abdomen and pulled out a loop of his intestines.

Pete screamed at the top of his lungs.

Father Ed was watching the carnage from a shattered, boarded-up window. He pulled away with a sick look on his face, and turned toward the rest of the people in the room, shaking his head dolefully.

"They got him," he announced in a barely audible voice. "It's so awful. Don't none of you look."

Sister Hillary said, "May God have mercy on his immortal soul."

Bertie moaned, "We're gonna die...we're gonna die..."

Annie said, "Shut up, Bertie, you're making us all feel worse."

CHAPTER 16

As the poker game was coming to an end after four rugged hours of it, Doc Holliday and Sheriff Parkman had driven the others out and had a roughly equal share of the chips. The losers, Heck and Wyatt, had sat there observing, drinking and smoking for the past few hands.

"Wanna draw for high card?" Doc Holliday asked the sheriff. "Let's get this thing over with."

"I don't wanna go boom or bust," said the sheriff. "Everybody else had their chances same as you and I did. Rules of the game say you and me can agree to stop whenever we want to, and call ourselves winners."

"I'll agree to that if you want to chicken out," Doc Holliday said.

"Not chickening out, just living to fight another day," said the sheriff.

They both gathered their chips into little cloth pouches and went to the bar to exchange them for cold cash.

Wild Bill said, with a dour look on his face, "I've gotta ask one of 'em to lend me a hundred bucks. If I go home totally broke Calamity will butcher me with a cleaver. Good thing I already handed her the cash she wanted for wine and groceries."

"That's 'cause she was smart enough to grab it while the grabbin' was good," Heck said with a chuckle.

"I'll lend you the hundred," Wyatt Earp offered. "I always hold something in reserve. Like the gold pieces in my vest pocket."

Doc Holliday and Sheriff Parkman came back to the table tucking greenbacks into their pants pockets, and now the gamblers were ready to just relax and top off their drinks.

Wyatt eyed the sheriff in all seriousness and said to him, "Doc and I came here because we heard about the savagery you've been dealing with. It sounds really bad even if it's only half true. We'd be happy to lend a hand if you need us."

Raising his eyebrows, Heck said, "You know about the cannibalism? We didn't think it was getting out all over."

"I suppose it isn't, but we have our sources," said Wyatt. "Doc even has some theories as to what might be at work here."

"We know one thing that's at work," Heck Thomas said. "A fucking Lakota medicine man and a passel of so-called Ghost Dancers."

Doc Holliday said, "That factor has to do with superstition, not science, and I don't believe you should totally buy into it. Back in the Dark Ages, folks didn't know what a total eclipse was, and so they did all kinds of crazy things out of their belief that the world was going to end."

"Listen to Doc, he always knows what he's talking about," Wyatt advised. "He has several degrees, not just in dentistry. He studied at a famous college in Philadelphia."

"You two have been places," the sheriff said to Wyatt and Doc. "If the doc has any worthwhile theories, I'd certainly give them a listen."

"Did you gentlemen ever hear of scrapie?" Doc Holliday asked.

Looking utterly perplexed, they shook their heads no.

Doc said, "To become a dentist you have to earn a medical degree first, before you get to learn the more mechanical procedures. I had a college roommate who didn't want to be anything but a medical research scientist, and in one of his classes he learned about a sheep disease called scrapie. He was of the belief that in certain circumstances, it could acquire the ability to infect humans, not just animals. It's a disease we've known about for over a century, but have not learned how to cure it."

"What are the symptoms?" Heck asked.

"Well, one of the clinical signs is that infected sheep will compulsively scrape off their fleece by rubbing against rocks, trees or fences. They also exhibit excessive lip smacking, altered gaits, and convulsions. It appears to be caused by enigmas in the brain, which we don't yet understand, but they are called *prions*."

"Come again?" said Sheriff Parkman. He wasn't sure he was totally following what Doc Holliday was explaining, but he felt it was somehow important.

Doc said, "Prions are proteins in the brain that can be seen to have become folded in on themselves, under a microscope. They accumulate in the infected animal's body, especially in the nerve cells, then the nerve cells die. Along the way toward eventual death, in sheep, some of the more extreme symptoms include tremor, a shambling walk like one sees in cases of rabies, and an urge to bite into their own legs and feet."

"I'll be damned!" Sheriff Parkman blurted. "What if a human form of this scrapie thing would cause some of the sufferers to start biting into other folks as well as themselves?"

Doc said, "You've hit the nail on the head, Sheriff. As strange as it sounds, to me it's a rather strong possibility."

"It would account for the cannibalism," Heck said. "But the ones I've battled with aren't just sick -- they're *dead*."

"Scrapie can be transmitted to herds of deer, "Doc Holliday pointed out. "As a matter of fact, at times it's been called Zombie Deer Disease."

"Wow," Heck murmured to himself, realizing the irony.

Wyatt said, "There are a lot more sheep ranchers than their used to be, in spite of the way the cattlemen tried to drive them out. Scrapie might've taken hold in one of their herds, and when those infected animals got eaten, people might have come down with a human form of it."

"But a disease can be dealt with in animals, even if entire herds have to be shot and buried," said Doc Holliday. "But we can't do that to human beings."

"We can if we're attacked," Heck said. "I already done it."

"And with my blessing," said the sheriff. "But, Doc, where does the Ghost Dancing come in, if this is a medical problem?"

Doc Holliday said, "The Bubonic Plague was made to spread faster and be much more lethal by entire congregations anointing themselves with infected Holy Water. Superstition isn't always harmless, in fact far from it. I suspect the Ghost Dancers are well on their way to being agents of their own destruction."

CHAPTER 17

Jed Harris and Danielle Greer were riding side by side across a field toward a pond, where they dismounted and let their horses drink.

Jed said, "This mare is easy to handle. I thought she'd give a hard time 'cause she's not mine."

"She's gentle because she was broke in for my young niece, Letty. She's in one of the four graves we saw. The saddle was hers too."

"That makes me really sad, just to think about her. If I survive, I'll make sure to pray for her every day."

They both got down on their knees, scooped up water with their hands, and drank. Danielle stood up first while Jed splashed water on his face.

Danielle said, "Even if we get to the school and they're desperate for help, I don't think we can rescue them all by ourselves. You don't even have your gun."

"Let's just check the situation out," Jeff said after thinking it over. "They may be all right. Might have the place boarded up tight. Or maybe they got out of there in time."

She said, "I doubt it. Chances are they got taken totally unawares, like you did.

He wanted to cry, thinking about Barney, but he didn't want to look weak in front of her. He choked it back and managed to say, "My poor dog. He died trying to protect me, I'm sure of that. We were like brothers, me and him. He was nine years old and I had him all that time."

She stepped closer to him and embraced him, and he gave in to it, realizing it was the best and most welcome hug he had ever gotten.

CHAPTER 18

Sheriff Parkman spoke to Nocona through the bars of his cell.

"Two Lakota are outside waiting for you, Mr. Medicine Man. They ain't doin' no Ghost Dance, they're just waiting. They're Indian Police. They told me twenty-three of your whatchacallem -- your *disciples* -- were attacked, blasted down and carved up, and it was done by your twin brother, Otarro, and his bunch of nut cases. They also back up what you tried to convince me of, that your teachings are peaceful, even though I think they're delusional. So I'm gonna open this cell door and make you a free man -- for now. You better not do anything that makes me change my mind."

Nocona said grimly but insistently, "I want to help hunt him down -- my brother, the evil one of us two. He should have been killed as he left my mother's womb. He deserves that, and it should happen now, and as soon as possible."

Sheriff Parkman said, "I wouldn't cry over him if that happens, no matter who or what makes it happen. Just don't let me catch you at it."

So saying, he unlocked the cell and escorted Nocona outside, where two Indian Police, Red Feather and Bold Eagle, were waiting on the wooden porch. They wore white wide-brimmed hats with feathers in their hat bands, and, true to his name, Red Feather's was red. Their blue uniforms bore the insignia of the Lakota Indian Police. In spite of their close association with the Deadwood sheriff and his deputies, they still wore their black hair long and chopped off, like others of their tribe.

Sheriff Parkman said, "Well, here's your revered leader, with no pending charges against him unless he fucks up."

Red Feather instantly countered what the sheriff just said, and in no uncertain terms. "Nocona is not a leader over Bold Eagle nor me. We are not Ghost Dancers. We are Lakota loyalists who try our best to enforce our laws. And the laws of White people when your own laws mirror ours."

Bold Eagle said, "Even now, our scouts are tracking the wicked Otarro and his gang of murderers and rapists. We will punish them much more severely than your laws permit."

"Well, good luck to you, then," Sheriff Parkman said in all sincerity.

He watched as Bold Eagle and Red Feather got on their horses, and Nocona mounted the extra one they had brought for him. He lingered till they got a long way down the dusty street of his town. Then he turned and went back into his office and jail.

Sitting behind his plank desk, he put his feet up and put a chunk of chew in his mouth as he thought things over, particularly what Doc Holliday had said about the sheep disease called Scrapie. He didn't need anyone to figure out for him that it had gotten that name from the way infected animals scraped their fleece off till the flesh bled. But he didn't have the mind of a scientist, so it was a total mystery to him as to whether or not that damned sheep disease could somehow be transmitted to humans.

And what about those distorted -- or perverted -- prions in the animals' brains?

The sheriff could imagine such a thing turning folks into ravenous cannibals on their way to an early death.

He just didn't know if it could actually be a true cause of the cannibalistic attacks by people who no longer *looked* human. In fact, they already looked dead.

CHAPTER 19

A pack of zombies waded into a creek far enough that they could, without bending or stooping, use their hands to scoop water and drink it. The ragged nondescript clothes that they wore, including their ghost shirts, were spattered with dried blood and specks of flesh from their latest human victims.

Otarro and four of his Comancheros chuckled as they looked down on the zombies from a wooden bridge over the creek. Without a word, he took aim, picking out the first zombie that he wanted to bring down. As he got the dead creature in his sights, the other desperadoes followed suit. Then, when Otarro fired his first shot, the others took his cue and started firing, too.

They continued their fusillade for a long time, fully enjoying it. Their high-powered rifles blasted holes clean through every part of the dead things' bodies, sending pieces of nearly bloodless flesh flying everywhere around them.

When Otarro and his gang galloped back across the bridge, their horses' hooves clattering ferociously on the wooden boards, they left zombie carcasses floating in the creek.

CHAPTER 20

Sister Hillary assembled the scared little flock of children in the chapel at St. Willard's, and Father Ed entered to lead them in prayer. The kindly priest was keenly aware of his responsibility to save as many lives as he could, should worse come to worst, and he knew the calming influence of prayer, not only by virtue of its communication with God and his saints, but also, psychologically, by virtue of simple concentration and repetition.

Unfortunately, though some of these well-thought-out tactics worked with most of the children, and even with Janice Kimble and Sister Hillary, it had little effect on little Bertie Samuels, who was in a back pew, crying and moaning, with Annie Kimball attempting to console him. Father Ed constantly had to admire her good judgment, especially for a thirteen-year-old. She knew how to try to be helpful without needing to be told to do it.

"Let us pray," Father Ed said, once he got everybody kneeling, except for Bertie. Then he led them all in the Lord's Prayer. "Our Father, who art in heaven, hallowed be Thy Name. Thy kingdom come, thy will be done, on earth as it is in heaven. Give us this day our daily bread, and forgive us our trespasses, as we forgive those who trespass against us. And lead us not into temptation, but deliver us from evil. Amen."

Father Ed could recite the Lord's Prayer by rote, so his mind wandered even as he was saying it, but the meanderings had to do with how the words might be applied to the present situation. For instance, was the Lord's Kingdom already at hand? Were the dead being awakened, according to the biblical pronouncements in the Book of Revelations?

Were all the Doomsday Prophecies now coming true in a most horrific way?

Some people who called themselves Christians actually fervently hoped for it all to hurry up and happen. They longed for the return of Jesus Christ, when, according to the Bible, his earthly reign would begin. He would vanquish all evil, and allow those who were free of sin to live alongside him in peace and harmony. Then he would "rapture" them into Heaven.

But Father Ed desperately did not want to believe that the civilization he knew would come to an end that way. He wanted to be rescued. He wished for all of the members of his little flock to be saved -- not in the biblical sense -- but in the earthly sense of being free to live out their lives.

CHAPTER 21

Nocona and his two Indian Police escorts, Bold Eagle and Red Feather, were riding their horses through a spectacularly beautiful rustic terrain bordered by low hills green with trees and vegetation.

But they didn't know that Otarro and five of his Comancheros had concealed themselves at the top of one of those hills. Their horses tethered out of sight, they were lying flat on their stomachs with a perfect vantage point to sight in on the three riders below.

Suddenly, they let loose with a devastating fusillade, instantly killing Red Feather and Bold Eagle, tumbling them from their saddles. Red Feather hit the ground with a thud, stone cold dead, but Bold Eagle's boot caught in his stirrup, and he was dragged by his horse, screaming till he finally died, as the horse fled.

But Nocona managed to ride on, even though bullets had struck his right shoulder and his left thigh. He whipped his horse with its reins and dug his heels in, trying as hard as he could to get out of danger, as Otarro and the five other attackers galloped down from the hill where they had been hiding.

Otarro yelled at the top of his lungs, "Hold your fire! Take him alive!"

Nocona had a lead on them that was diminishing rapidly. He whipped his horse, groaning from pain and loss of blood.

His pursuers were gaining fast and closing in.

Weak and dizzy, Nocona fell from his horse in a cloud of dust -- and the horse kept on galloping.

Otarro rode up upon Nocona's body as the cloud of dust around it cleared.

He saw that his birth brother was not dead. Though Nocona was bleeding badly from his wounds, he managed to crawl a short distance, then rolled over in the dirt, looking up at his evil brother. He murmured in agony. "Otarro...I...I..."

"Don't talk or I will cut your tongue out!" Otarro barked. "I should have done so long ago!"

CHAPTER 22

Not long after the poker game ended and the gamblers started into some serious drinking, Doc Holliday caught a lung full of acrid smoke from Wild Bill's cigar and was overcome by a coughing fit. He yanked a big white handkerchief from his breast pocket, coughed into it, stared at it and saw a gob of thick blood. Then he put it to his mouth again because he couldn't stop coughing.

Wyatt Earp patted his back hard and said, "Are you all right?" But the coughing still wouldn't come to an end.

Doc appreciated Earp's concern, knowing it was heartfelt because Wyatt always said they were friends for life after Doc saved Wyatt's life in a gun duel.

"Put out that goddamn cigar!" Wyatt yelled at Wild Bill. "Can't you see how my good friend here is suffering?"

To his credit, Wild Bill stubbed his cigar out and tossed it into a spittoon.

More coughing and more blood soaked Doc's big white handkerchief, and he had to excuse himself from the table.

"Want me to go with you?" Wyatt asked.

But Doc shook his head no, and half walked, half staggered to the Golden Nugget Hotel, where he climbed the stairs to his room, couldn't wait to get it unlocked, and coughed more bloody mucus into the bowl of water on a side table, then fell into bed in total agony.

His mother had died of tuberculosis when he was a fifteen-year-old boy, in Georgia, and his sister had died of it before he was born. He came down with it at age twenty, just as he had earned his degree in dentistry, and he likely acquired the disease from being his mother's caretaker. In fact, he was so ill that, after trying to work his dental practice in various places down South, he headed out West where the climate might be beneficial. He went from Missouri to Texas, and then Arizona, sometimes still trying to ply his trade as a dentist, and other times resorting to gambling and card dealing in various saloons and casinos.

He never allowed himself to sink into self-pity; instead he tried to live the way he wanted to, and with no regrets. He wasn't a womanizer because he didn't want to wish his disease on them. But he did manage to have an on-again off-again girlfriend, Mary Horony, a dance hall gal and occasional prostitute whose nickname was "Big Nose Kate." He knew her to be "tough, stubborn and fearless," which was the way he sometimes described her. He said she was highly educated but chose to work as a prostitute because she liked her independence. He couldn't help wishing she was here, taking care of him as he lay in bed. But he had left her behind in Dallas.

He was perspiring profusely, soaking his mattress, and, at the same time, was being wracked with chills and tremors. When he at long last fell into a fitful sleep, tossing and turning, he suffered crazy, distorted nightmares.

The nightmares were about dead people chasing after him, or scraping their naked bodies against boulders and log fences till their skin was torn and bleeding.

When he awoke in the middle of the night, it was dark outside his window, but he had no idea what time it was. Had he slept for four hours, or two days? He did not know. He wished his friend Wyatt would come and knock on the door and help him straighten his mind out. He felt weak and dissipated, but gratified that he was no longer coughing. Sometimes he had welcome stretches where he almost felt well, and that was when he could carry on with his life as if he was normal for just a little while.

He remembered some of the ugly, fearful content of his nightmares and realized they were fueled, at least in part, by the discussion in the saloon about dead people and scrapie.

He wished he had a full life ahead of him, but he knew that he didn't. The tuberculosis would take him. If it weren't for his disease, he thought he would like to do some scientific research. The discovery he had told the other gamblers about, the prions in the brains of sheep, that were like gaps in their mentality, might have ramifications for humans. Perhaps it was a cause of mental illness. Perhaps even a cause of the types of rage that turned men into savage killers.

Doc thought that if people were seeming to be dead and hungering for human flesh, it could be that their bestial urges, kept dormant in most folks, could unfold when the gaps made by the prions took over.

He regretted that he would probably never get to pursue his curiosity about all of it unless his own disease would be cured someday while he was still alive to reap the benefits.

But while he was still above ground, he would do his best to help Sheriff Parkman deal with the plague, or whatever he wanted to call it, whether it was caused by Ghost Dancers or folded prions or a combination of both factors.

CHAPTER 23

Jed and Danielle had dismounted during their long trek, and were leading their horses as they walked.

Jed said, "Let's get back on 'em. I can feel blisters on my feet. We shouldn't have backtracked so much."

Danielle said, "I was hoping to find people who could help us, but no such luck. The horses are darn near worn out, and I guess it's partly my fault. But no matter how you cut it they need a break from carrying us. You want 'em to collapse?"

"Heaven forbid! But where can we get guns? If we reach the school unarmed, we won't be able to do much, no matter what kind of trouble we find there."

"There's an army trading post up ahead," Danielle said. "I know they sell shotguns, rifles and a few handguns -- if they're not overrun. And if they're shut up tight with the troopers gone, having abandoned the place, we might have to bust our way in."

Grimacing, Jed said, "That's if a pack of zombies didn't bust in ahead of us."

He knew his blisters would start bursting, if they hadn't already, and then they would hurt worse and might get infected. But Danielle was right. They had to keep walking. They'd be in even worse shape if their horses collapsed on them.

He was liking Danielle more and more as they worked together toward the same goal, which was to survive, and also help the people who might be under siege at the school, especially the innocent children.

Jed hoped to have children someday. He wasn't the typical young bachelor, always on the hunt but never ready to settle down, never ready to live with the same woman in a lengthy marriage with all the obligations of a wife and kids. Sometimes he felt somehow too tame, polite or decent, or else that young women might not think he was as masculine as those other guys. He had often been perturbed by the fact that the girls seemed to go for rougher, cruder guys even if it wasn't in their best interests. And when they married these types, seeing them as protectors, they often turned out to be just the opposite -- in other words, abusers.

These kinds of thoughts made Jed determined to prove himself to Danielle no matter what happened. He didn't want her to stick him in a pigeonhole. He didn't think he was lot braver than most people. But he didn't want to come off as a coward.

CHAPTER 24

Nocona was sitting up in the bed of a wagon, looking more alert than he was when he was first shot. His shoulder and leg had been bandaged by someone while he was unconscious; he didn't know who did it, and he could barely bring himself to care; he thought it was like brushing a condemned man's teeth before putting a noose around his neck. There were ropes around his check and arms, binding him to a rail of the wagon bed.

Otarro came up behind him for the shock value, snickered, then handed him a canteen. He considered that to be more false mercy. He spat at Otarro, but missed, and Otarro chortled.

"Do you hate me, my brother?" Otarro asked impishly. "I wanted to torture you, and then skin you alive. But I pride myself on my pragmatism as well as my viciousness. I think your Ghost Dancers would pay all the money they have to get you back. They are lost without you. They are ragged and destitute but they will beg, borrow and steal for you. I am going to demand ten thousand dollars from them. Perhaps even some of the White men will chip in, since you haven't scalped any of them."

Nocona said, "They won't give you money. They will find you and shoot you down like a mangy dog."

"Hah!" scoffed Otarro. "My Comancheros are battle hardened, used to living on boiled leather when they have to, whereas the blue-bellies are soft. They do not wish to be mired in another sea of mud, killing and eating their own horses. If they should get stuck like rabbits stuck in tar, we will ride around them laughing as we shoot them full of arrows."

CHAPTER 25

Jed and Danielle at last reached the U.S. Army Trading Post, but remained on foot, leading their mounts as they approached it cautiously.

They felt extremely uneasy because there didn't seem to be any human activity whatsoever. When they got close enough, they tethered their horses to hitching posts in front of the large unpainted plank building.

By this time, they had already noticed that the front door was hanging off its hinges, wide open. And when they stepped up onto the broad porch, they saw three skeletal, totally devoured bodies so badly ravaged that their calves were chewed to the bone, and their arms looked to have been pulled nearly out of their sockets.

Gasping in alarm, Jed said, "Holy hell! A pack of those things must've torn them apart!"

"It's so ghastly I don't want to look," Danielle said. "But the zombies, if that's what we need to be calling them, are after human flesh, not guns. I don't think guns mean a darn thing to them. So there might be guns in there yet."

"Cover me with your rifle," Jed said, "if you still have any ammo in it. All I have is my screwdriver. I'm scared of whatever might jump out at me."

"The place seems dead, no pun intended. If you go in, I'm going in with you."

They warily entered the building, and when they encountered no immediate danger, they found their way to a large gun cabinet displaying weapons for sale.

"Excellent!" Danielle exclaimed. "Stand back, Jed!"

She slammed the glass front of the display case with the butt of her rifle. Careful not to cut himself on splintered shards, Jed seized a double-barreled shotgun and a lever-action rifle, then handed Danielle a Confederate Navy Colt, which was a .36 caliber imitation of the Union's .45 caliber in the same basic design.

He said, "Let's go through these drawers, Danielle. Look for ammunition -- the different kinds we need."

"Gladly, honey...I mean --"

She didn't mean for that word, 'honey', to slip out.

She and Jed eyed one another, both embarrassed.

"I mean...I guess...I guess we've been through so much together," she said querulously.

"Yeah, it feels like I've known you for a while," he managed to say, a bit unsure of what he exactly meant.

Was he falling for her? That notion felt sort of scary and strange. And it felt even stranger to think of how she had called him "honey." She had said it was a slip of her tongue. But he had liked hearing it, and he kept rolling it around in his head as they hurried out of the trading Post, secured their weapons and mounted their horses.

With her boots in the stirrups and the reins in her hands, she smiled and said, "I'm scared, but I'm having fun. Am I goofy?"

"Fun?!" he blurted, adjusting his rump in his saddle.

She said, "Up until a couple of weeks ago, I was sedately and safely *bored* in a boarding school called Bridgerton Academy, near Cleveland. And now I'm in an actual adventure and loving the excitement. We called it a *boring* school instead of a boarding school."

They were going easy on their mounts instead of pushing them too hard, anxious to get to the church and school but not wanting to make their desperation worse by having to abandon their horses and keep going on foot.

"Things out here are rough, but it's where I grew up," Danielle said. "I was supposedly getting a good education at Bridgerton, but I felt boxed in, trying to act like a debutant when I felt more like a tomboy. I'll tell you about it sometime."

Once again his feelings for her stirred, at the implication that she might want to see more of him after their "adventure," as she had called it, was over.

As they rode on, while Jed dared to mull over romantic possibilities, she thought about the friends she missed from her days at Bridgerton, but also about the things she didn't like. Just about as soon as she arrived, all her personal things were gone through. She was given about one minute to say goodbye to her father. He hugged her, kissed her cheek and wished her farewell, then headed for a hotel and got on a train the next morning. The train wouldn't take him all the way back to Deadwood. He'd have to go the last hundred or so miles by stagecoach. She wouldn't see him for a year, during which time she would turn eighteen, while being transformed into a "polite and cultured young lady."

Her dormitory was a plain, unadorned room for one hundred and fifty girls, without walls between beds. A governess had her own room at one end. Each girl had a white metal bed and a small white night table with one drawer. An older girl tutored them on how to make perfect beds, and if anyone's bed was sloppy they all had to tear their sheets off and remake them. They were told this was the way things were done in the finest boarding schools in London.

Each morning, they were served two cooked prunes, a bowl of oatmeal, and milk and toast, the same things each and every day. Governesses monitored the way they used their utensils. If they did anything wrongly, they were "corrected", and told "nice girls don't do it that way."

The overriding goal of the Academy was to instill "ladylike behavior." Danielle, along with all the other girls in her class, had to learn not just proper etiquette, but also sewing, crocheting, embroidering, darning and mending. She was taught how to set a table, how to be a hostess, and how to engage in the art of conversation that would always be polite and never offensive in any way.

There were no boys or men, except for one elderly maintenance man, and the girls were not permitted to talk with him. At night, she secretly thought of roughnecks back home that she had had budding crushes on.

Amid the clatter of hooves while they were riding, she said to Jed, "I couldn't wait to get the hell out of there. And that's putting it mildly."

"Didn't you make any friends?"

"Well, yes, but we were watched all the time, so we never got to really know each other except superficially. Like I said, I'll tell you all about it sometime."

She wanted to tell him how she was made fun of by a clique of snooty rich girls from New York who found out she was the daughter of a saloon keeper. One of them claimed to be related to a Vanderbilt, and the clique fawned over her. Danielle would've liked to tear their hair out, but she had had to rein herself in so she wouldn't disappoint her father by getting expelled. She wished she didn't have to be so damned sedate all the time. Snooty people didn't last long where she came from. She was brought up on a ranch run by her mother after her parents separated, and she was only nine when her mother died of diphtheria, then she was taken in by her father. She knew he loved her and had sent her to Bridgerton Academy because he thought he was doing his best for her. "I have the money," he said, "and if you get a good education, you won't be dependent on nobody."

She had to reluctantly admit she felt more well-rounded by the time she came home to Deadwood.

But she still couldn't picture herself crocheting.

She decided that, from now on, she would be "sedate and proper" when she felt it was called for, and at other times she would enjoy being her true self.

CHAPTER 26

The adults and children who had barricaded themselves at St. Willard's church and school were behaving in erratic ways now, due to their extreme fright and uncertainty. Some were relatively calm, but others were pacing around, fidgeting or crying, scared out of their wits.

Others had never left the chapel after joining in on the Lord's Prayer. They were still kneeling down, as badly as their knees hurt from doing it for so long, each mumbling whatever prayers suite them, whether liturgical or made up on the spot.

Father Ed, Annie Kimble and Annie's mother, Janice, were in the school room, half afraid to look at the boarded-up windows or the torn-apart desks. A couple of the littlest kids were there, sticking close to Father Ed as their protector. Annie was hugging the perpetual whiner, Bertie Samuels, trying to keep him from wailing some more.

Suddenly they heard muffled hoof beats.

Annie jumped up and looked out the window nearest her. "Someone's coming!" she cried out. "Look, Father Ed!"

He joined Annie at the window and said, "It looks like Kyle Samuels"

"Hooray! It's my daddy!" Bertie yelled.

He leapt up and dashed to a window, anxious to catch sight of his father. There was enough moonlight that he could realize it was really his father, halting his horse at the edge of the woods surrounding the church and school, then dismounting and grabbing an unlit lantern that was hanging from the pommel of his saddle.

"I'm coming in!" he yelled. "They're afraid of fire! Get ready to unlock the door!"

He struck a wooden stove match and lit the kerosene lantern, turning up the flame till it was bright and hot. Then he pulled a revolver from his waistband and ventured out into the school yard with the gun in his right hand and the lantern in his left.

All went well for about twenty paces, Kyle inching forward, scared and warily glancing all around.

Bertie watched from one window, peering between the boards nailed over it, while Annie and Father Ed watched from another boarded-up window.

Kyle kept coming, hunkered down, stepping up his pace toward the building. But zombies were now closing in on him from behind him and from two sides, and he didn't see the ones from behind.

He got to within two feet of the door, and Father Ed hastened to unlock it for him.

But Kyle didn't make it! He was set upon by three of the zombies, and he fired his gun twice at one of them. One shot went wild, but the second one hit the zombie in the head and the creature went down.

Kyle started to aim at yet another zombie -- but the gun was knocked out of his hand.

Two more zombies clutched Kyle by his throat and right arm.

With his left arm he swung the lantern at them -- but a ghoulish arm blocked it and swiped at it, and Kyle lost his grip. It fell to the ground, still burning.

A leering female zombie stooped and picked up the lantern.

She swung it at the window that Bertie was peering through.

CRASH!

Glass shattered, and the lantern went through the window, landing on the floor of the classroom in a puddle of flaming kerosene.

Bertie was on fire and *screaming!* He bolted for the door and tried to yank it open -- but Father Ed tripped him and yelled, "Annie! Get something to smother the flames on him! Not a bucket of water -- that'll make it worse!"

Annie grabbed a coat hanging in the cloakroom, ran over to Bertie, who was screaming in total agony, covered him up and tried to smother the flames.

The whole room was on fire -- and so was Janice Kimble.

Sister Hillary took over Annie's efforts to save Bertie while Annie ran to her own mom, saw that only small patches of her clothes were on fire, and almost dove on her and tried to smother the intermittent flames with her own body.

But Janice wasn't moving.

Annie cried out, "Oh, my God! It's her heart! I think she's gone!

Father Ed and Sister Hillary stopped Annie from throwing herself down on Janice's body. She must not have been hit with much kerosene because the small patches of flame had gone out and were only smoldering.

But a large part of the wooden floor and parts of the walls were now starting to burn ferociously.

Father Ed yelled, "Quick, everybody! We've gotta get out! The back door!"

"But my mom!" Annie cried.

Sister Hillary said, "We can't do anything for her now, Annie. She's not one of us anymore."

As if on cue, Janice sat up.

Annie was frozen in her tracks, wanting to hug her mother, yet knowing she shouldn't.

Sister Hillary pulled Annie away. They followed everybody else to the back door. Father Ed led the way out by moving quickly to the log pile and arming himself with a slender but stout log to use as a club. Two zombies were immediately upon him, and he bashed one of them in the face. The zombie fell, its countenance shattered, and it writhed and kicked and gurgled on the ground, like a wounded animal.

But several of the children didn't have a chance. They got pulled down and swarmed over by ghouls.

The rest of the people, led by Father Ed and Sister Hillary, managed to run toward the woods. But two more children got pounced on by zombies who leapt on them from behind trees and bushes.

The survivors kept running, hoping to find some semblance of safety, however temporary.

A half dozen zombies pursued them, shambling in their slow, rigor-mortis-inhibited gait, drooling and hissing hungrily.

CHAPTER 27

Doc Holliday knew his reputation as a gunslinger was largely fictional, built up and exaggerated by the tabloid newspapers and dime novels. In one way he didn't mind it, because most people feared him and left him alone; but on the other hand it put a target on his back.

He had come West to deal with his disease, not to kill people. For God's sake, he was a dentist! He hadn't gone through a strenuous education because he thought he would make a lot of money; he had basically wanted to *help* people. Why couldn't they understand that?

They'd be stunned if they knew that right at this moment, in the middle of an assault on humanity by transmogrified humans, their big bad gunslinger was spending a lot of time in Deadwood's town library, researching what scientists had discovered, to this point, about the inner workings of the human brain. As he had hinted to Wyatt, Wild Bill and Sheriff Parkman in Jesse Grier's saloon, he had a strong notion that human beings that were -- or seemed to be -- dead were turning on other human beings.

It was certain that the sheep disease known as scrapie was caused by damaged prions that left gaps in the animals' brains, and therefore, if it mutated, it might cause that same kind of damage in people. Including the inclination to viciously devour their own kind.

Even long prior to this current year, 1876, in the midst of the Victorian Age, an intense inquiry, both scientific and pseudoscientific, had been launched, and was still being probed, into the workings of the human mind.

Doc Holliday thought that phrenology was merely a pseudoscience, but it was all the rage for decades. Its practitioners claimed that, by examining the bumps and valleys on their patients' heads, they could glean clues to who they would best fall in love with, the kind of parents they would be, what career path would be right for them, and so on and so forth. They were still writing books and preaching about their craft and convincing hordes of people to have their heads examined. Phrenology parlors and "automated phrenology machines' had popped up all over America and Europe.

This all got started in the late 1700's when a German physician, Franz Joseph Gall, noticed that people with larger eyes and more expansive foreheads seemed more adept at memorizing long passages. Thus he surmised that one's emotional characteristics were not dictated by the heart, as was assumed at the time, but from somewhere in the head. He postulated that the shape of the skull reflected personality traits and mental abilities that corresponded to the topography of the brain. He gave the name "phrenology" to his so-called "science of the mind."

People scrambled to attend phrenology lectures, and some of them even began to style their hair to show off their most pronounced head bumps. Dr. Gall propounded that pressure from the brain caused ridges or depressions on the outside of a person's skull, and that the location of these bumps and valleys could provide diagnosis of twenty-seven different behaviors and traits which he referred to as "faculties." He had mapped them by measuring people from all walks of life, including prisoners and mental patients. He especially liked to measure odd-shaped heads. For example, after examining the heads of young pickpockets, he purported to have discovered that many of them had bumps above their ears.

Upon reading this in a library book, Doc Holliday felt above his own ears -- and there were bumps. But he thought that almost everybody had them, so the trait wasn't as unusual as Dr. Gall wanted to believe.

Doc realized that modern science had revealed knowledge about the human brain that was more substantial than the quackery of phrenology. He read that when the human brain was damaged, the part that suffered most was the neocortex, the seat of complex logic and subtle reasoning. And, if and when it suffered a lesion, all sorts of unpredictable behavior regressions could result.

That night, after dinner at the Golden Nugget, the doc told his friend Wyatt about some of the deeply interesting things revealed by his research. Like himself, Wyatt Earp was a complex individual, which contributed to their friendship. He didn't try to stop Doc Holliday from expounding.

"The human brain is not just one complete organ," Doc explained. "There are three parts to it -- the limbic system, the reptile complex and the neocortex, which is the most primitive part. It's the reptilian side of us that is the seat of deception and aggression. When it isn't controlled by the neocortex, we become like primitive beasts, driven by urges to rape or kill or eat. In other words, to gratify whatever impulse we might feel at any given moment."

Wyatt said, "It certainly sounds like what Sheriff Parkman and Heck Thomas are dealing with. I think we should stick around and help them, old buddy."

"I do, too," said the Doc, "and I knew that's the way you would feel."

"Yep," said Wyatt. "They're dealing with Whites and Indians both that aren't human anymore. They're mindless monsters and they have to be put down."

CHAPTER 28

Danielle said, "Look at the smoke above those trees! That's exactly where St. Willard's is!"

"Oh-oh, I'm scared of what we might find," Jed said to her.

They spurred their mounts. By the time they got closer, they could peer between the trees and see fire. And when they burst into the clearing, they were dumbstruck by what they saw.

The church and school were being consumed by fire -- everything was almost gone.

Zombies were backing away from the flames and the heat, carrying pieces of human flesh.

Although Jed and Danielle couldn't recognize Janice Kimble because they hadn't known her, they could tell that, whoever she was, she had obviously been recently brought back from death by whatever was causing the "zombie disease."

Hungry zombies had crowded in on remnants of the children who were killed while trying to escape the fire. The undead were fighting over scraps of meat, like a pack of ravenous wolves.

Jed and Danielle were in shock.

He said, "There's nothing we can do here. Obviously they were overrun."

"But there would've been more of them. Where do you think they could've gone?'

"I don't think they were rescued. If that had happened, all of these zombies would've been gunned down."

"That's one thing we could do," Danielle said. "We have plenty of ammunition."

Jed said, "I'm with you. Let's get the bastards!"

He and Danielle got in close, still on their horses, and began gunning down the obliviously feasting ghouls. But they didn't stay oblivious for long. They got up and started backing away, growling and stumbling till they took bullets to their heads.

Jed and Danielle kept on shooting, vanquishing as many of the undead as they could.

Some of the zombies tried to escape into the woods. But Jed spurred his horse after them, on a wide, trampled-looking path. He shot two in the head. But three more escaped among the trees.

He heard more gunshots from somewhere behind him -- and glanced back to where he had last seen Danielle.

"Danielle, are you okay?" he called out.

She yelled back at him, "Yeah! I got two more of them! Do what you have to do! I'm reloading!"

Then Jed spotted something hanging from a shrub. He rode up to it, leaned from his saddle and plucked it up. It was a child's scapular, a religious necklace bestowed to each person who received the sacrament of Confirmation at around age twelve. Jed looked at it, then noticed the flattened-down weeds his horse had trod upon, along with broken branches and other evidence that quite a few people must have tramped through here.

He tracked the signs of people tromping through this part of the woods, down to a little stream that they must have waded across. He and his horse waded across too, and he saw that the evidence of trampled weeds continued on the other side.

He turned his horse around and went back to find Danielle, then showed her the scapular.

"Look. I found this," he said. "I saw tramped-down weeds and muddy footprints leading across a stream. Did you say a priest and nun run the school?"

"Yeah, Sister Hillary and Father Ed. Does it look like they may have led some of the kids somewhere?"

"I'd say so."

"We better try to find them."

"I agree. Damn! I hope they're still alive."

CHAPTER 29

Sheriff Parkman was sitting behind his crude plank desk. Wyatt Earp and Doc Holliday occupied the two wooden chairs in front of him, and Heck Thomas and Wild Bill were standing.

Wyatt said, "Sheriff, I think the doc here has a handle on what might be the root of the crazy stuff you're dealing with, including, believe it or not, the cannibalism."

"I'm willing to listen to anything at this point," the sheriff said. "I don't give a damn if it's religious, superstitious or supposedly scientific."

"Well," said Wyatt, "what the doc came up with is for sure scientific. He can't prove it, but it makes total sense if you can cast all your previous thinking aside."

"All right. I'm all ears. Convince me."

"Go ahead, Doc," Wyatt said.

"Okay," the doc began. "I'm not just a dentist and I'm not just a crazy man with a six-shooter. To become an alumnus of a respected college in Philadelphia, I had to be at least reasonably intelligent. Right?"

The sheriff nodded and said, "Okay, I can believe that. But go on."

The doc proceeded to relate the same discoveries and theories he had divulged to his pal Wyatt a couple of hours ago.

As he wrapped up his discourse, Wild Bill said, "I admit I'm dumbfounded. What the hell do you other guys make of it?"

Heck said, "I think I pretty much follow you, Doc. You're a smart feller. In other words, you don't believe these flesh-hungry people are dead. They're brain damaged."

"Well, I suppose they might be dead as well, but can the *dead* be reanimated? I understand that Nocona and his Ghost Dancers want to believe they can be. But if so, it's something beyond contemporary science."

"I'll settle for brain damage as the explanation," Sheriff Parkman flatly said. "If they're dead, partly dead, or still alive and brain damaged, it don't matter to me. Because they still need to be exterminated."

"And that's a fact we can all agree on," said Wyatt.

"I hate to tell you," Sheriff Parkman said, "but I've got a big problem right here and now. Nobody in town has heard a peep from Father Ed at his church and one-room school. He's got a telegraph set to stay in touch, and he used to do it just about every day. He was a telegraph operator when he served in the Union army. It's likely something really bad has happened to him and maybe his school kids."

Heck said, "The telegraph company sent out a young feller named Jed Harris, one of their repairmen, in case the line needed to be fixed, -- and now the line is still dead and neither the company nor anybody else we know of has seen or heard neither hide nor hair of Jed."

"I can't deal with it all, just me and Heck and Billy," said the sheriff. "I need help from you and Doc, Wyatt, and I hope you're both willing."

"I would be," said Doc Holliday.

"So would I," Wyatt agreed.

"I'm glad to hear it," Sheriff Parkman said with a sigh of relief. "Lots of crazy shit has been goin' on, and I don't know why, in spite of what Doc Holiday has said. Seems to me it's also all mixed up with the Ghost Dancer thing. Nocona told a wild story about an evil brother of his bringing the dead back to life."

Wyatt said, "I'm not saying I believe dead people can come back to life, but I do believe bad things are being done by bad people."

"Well, look, we can't piss around," said the sheriff. "We have to go and rescue them kids at the school with the priest and nun. I don't want to go galloping out there with a thirty-man posse -- that'd for sure cause panic here in town. But you four gentlemen are experienced scouts, bounty hunters, and gunfighters. I wanna deputize all of you."

Wild Bill said, "Of course I'm in. But my wife will want to join in too."

The sheriff said, "I see no harm in that. Do you, Heck?"

"Well, Wyatt and Doc need to know for sure she can ride and shoot. I scouted right alongside of her and I can swear she's damned good. Don't let her womanly side persuade you otherwise -- she's not always like she was when you met her in the saloon."

Wyatt said, "Don't worry, I could sense right away she's nobody to mess with."

Wild Bill laughed and said, "You damn well better believe it, Wyatt! See this big bruise right here on my forehead?" He pulled his hair aside to display it. "She cooked me a nice steak dinner just like she promised, but I said somethin' that hit her wrong after I drunk too much wine, and she smacked me upside my head with the skillet."

CHAPTER 30

As she tramped through the woods with the other survivors of the fire, Sister Hillary fought a premonition that she was not going to survive, and prayed that when the time came, she would honestly be ready to let the Lord's will be done.

She felt that she had finally fully accepted her calling after years of uncertainty about it, in fact about sixteen years after she had taken her vows. She had been confused about it even as a sixteen-year-old girl, when she would quiver in fear each night of the God who was bent on making her a nun.

Fifteen years of Catholic education had constantly exposed her, nay *indoctrinated* her, with how she was destined for a monastic life. The holy sisters and priests would say things like, "You have the calling and you should obey it. I was once like you. I thought I didn't want to be shackled, but once I accepted it, I was and still am in eternal peace."

Under this constant well-meaning barrage upon her sensibilities, not just from priests and nuns, but also from friends and family, she began to be ashamed of her desires for marriage and motherhood. She grew pained that the God who was supposed to love her was going to force the vocation upon her, to *sanctify* her.

She failed to grow in love with Jesus Christ and learn who he truly was. She didn't tell anyone she had secretly shoved God to the back of her mind and had gone numbly into a convent with an attitude that since He was making her be a nun, she might as well bite the bullet. Ironically, she still believed that the religious life, for her, was the only route to holiness.

When she dared to confide this to the Mother Superior, it evoked a knowing smile from her, and after a long pause, she said, "My dear, don't feel that you have to stay here. You don't have to be a nun. And if you think that the Church or God *need* you, please do us a favor and leave."

Like a blow from a hammer, those words destroyed Sister Hillary's ego. In a strange, unforeseen way, they freed her. And now that she did not feel so *frightfully obligated* any more, she began to love God more easily.

It was a proud and definitely holy day in her life when she shed her maiden name of Patricia Summers and took the name of an ancient saint named Hillary. She had desired to adopt the name of her favorite female martyr, Saint Perpetua, who had been crucified by the ancient Romans. But she was admonished that nuns must always choose to name themselves after *male* saints, so she settled on Saint Hillary, who had been gored and ravaged by wild beasts in the Coliseum, then had his throat slit by gladiators.

These memories were still tumbling through Sister Hillary's mind when she, along with Father Ed, Annie Kimble and three other children reached a fairly large clearing and Father Ed halted them for a breather. They were all carrying sticks of various sizes that might be used as spears or clubs, but the ones in the hands of the smallest kids weren't of any great potential effectiveness.

Father said, "This won't be a good place for long. They can probably sniff us out. We've got to find shelter, someplace reasonably safe."

Sister Hillary said, "If we *could* camp here, and *if* we had guns, it'd be a good defensive position, wouldn't it? We can see all around the perimeter."

Ironically to her way of thinking, Father Ed said, "You sound like some sort of military strategist, Sister. Perhaps you missed your calling."

She had never mentioned, and didn't say so now, that she had come from a military family. Her father had been a Catholic chaplain, thus inaugurating the pressure on her to become a nun.

She said, "I wanted to work for peace, not war. I spent a lot of time on army posts, growing up."

Father Ed said, "Then for sure you'd recognize the fact that no army squad could camp in the open like this, especially without armed sentries, trip wires and mines."

Annie was scared, grieving for her mother, and impatient with the other two adults. She said, "What're we gonna do *now*, Father Ed?"

He answered, "We've got no choice. We've got to move on and hope we somehow encounter rescuers, or at least find someplace where we're reasonably protected and can hunker down."

Annie said, "That's what we tried to do back there, and it didn't work. Why don't we try to make it out to the main road? Maybe we'll find a farmhouse with people inside. Maybe they'll have guns."

"We can't straggle much farther," Father Ed countered. "We're at least two miles from any kind of main travel route, and these little kids can't move fast. They're worn out and badly frightened."

"Well, so am I," said Annie.

Father Ed could hardly blame her because he was frightened too. He had seen more than his share of carnage in the Civil War, and he had never wanted to see anything like it ever again. That was why he never would have volunteered for missionary work in some of the countries where priests were routinely tortured and killed while trying to convert people or else just teach them modern principles of cleanliness, water purification, or raising crops.

He never wanted to be a battlefield nurse, like his favorite poet, Walt Whitman. But even as a telegraph officer, he had been compelled to help in the aftermath of some of the bloodiest battles when the surgical tents were overflowing, and arms and legs had to be sawed off without any such thing as an anesthetic. He had seen bodies decapitated or ripped in half by cannons that fired iron balls linked together by chains, which could decimate an entire squad of soldiers all at once.

He had known first sergeants and young lieutenants who were gutsy and highly confident in their ability to lead. But Father Ed had self-doubts. He had been driven to enlist in order to help save the country given to him by its forefathers, but he had wished to be basically a noncombatant.

He had had the good luck to have made it through the war without losing life or limb, only to be plunged into a nightmare no one could ever have expected.

CHAPTER 31

Jed and Danielle were still trying to track the people that they thought may have escaped from the church and school. They were exhausted, the weapons they were carrying were heavy, their faces were sweaty and pasted with spider webs, and their necks and arms were itchy from insect bites.

Danielle said, "Maybe we should go back for our horses."

Surprised, Jed said, "You mean give up on a search for survivors?"

She thought about it for a second, then said, "No, I guess not. But maybe we'll find them dead in these woods. They could've stumbled into a pack of hungry ghouls."

"We haven't seen any evidence of that," Jeff pointed out to her. "There were plenty of chewed-up bodies back at the school, so the ghouls had their appetites tamped down, maybe. hard to imagine them taking the trouble to chase down a few people who took advantage of the situation to make a run for it."

"I hope you're right, Jed."

He scanned their immediate surroundings, looking for evidence of people passing through.

As tired as he was his eyes lit up and he said, "Look, Danielle! I almost didn't see that path over there because there's so much ground cover."

She said, "Good work, Hawkeye." Hawkeye being the name of the leading character in a novel by James Fennimore Cooper, who was portrayed as someone with skills and talents that Danielle had always thought were too preposterous.

CHAPTER 32

On the one hand, Calamity Jane was glad to be accepted by the men, and on the other hand she was used to it. She had been raised rough and was proud of the way she had made the most of it. After all, she had made it all the way from Princeton, Missouri, to Blackfoot, Montana, by wagon train when she was only thirteen, and on that trip she had learned how to drive a Conestoga and how to manage oxen. From Montana, she had headed to Fort Bridger, Wyoming, in charge of her five younger brothers and sisters because both of their parents had died on the first leg of their journey. She and her brood were some of the very first folks to ride on the Union Pacific train after a gold spike had been driven, in 1865, connecting the Eastern and Western parts of the nation.

By 1874, she was a scout for the army at Fort Russell, and in almost the same time period, she took occasional work as a prostitute at the Three Mile Hog Ranch near Fort Laramie, which was where she first met Billy Hickok, and both of them found out they were kindred spirits, both wild but both honest with one another.

She had fought and killed Indians and outlaws. And she figured these "ghouls", or whatever anyone wanted to call them, wouldn't be as tough as the bad guys and the marauding renegades, since they were essentially brain dead, according to Doc Holliday.

She'd bet Doc was missing his girlfriend, Big Nose Kate. He was handsome and she was comely and her nose wasn't really so big. Nobody should be making fun of her; she didn't deserve it, and she could be dangerous, too. Calamity respected Kate for sleeping with Doc, never minding about his bloody coughing spells. Did she think she was immune to tuberculosis? Or did she have some kind of death wish? Life on the plains was so excruciatingly dangerous, demanding and boring, sometimes for weeks and months on end, that many of the farm women couldn't take it, and committed suicide. Living in sod houses and hearing the constant whine of the wind and seeing nothing but constantly waving wheat sometimes drove them insane.

But no such thing was ever going to happen to Martha Jane Canary. She was determined to live up to her moniker, Calamity Jane. She was the dealer of calamities when she chose to be, not the recipient.

Wearing her leathers and well-armed with a rifle and two six-shooters, as well as a bowie knife in a sheathe on her leather belt, she rode with Billy into town, and they joined up with Wyatt, Doc, Heck Thomas and Sheriff Parkman, and their little posse was ready to head out for the Catholic church and schoolhouse, which was twenty-some miles away from Deadwood.

But Jesse Greer came huffing down the dirt street, dressed in the roughest clothes he owned and carrying an old-looking shotgun. "Hold up, Sheriff!" he called out. "I wanna go with you all!"

All the posse members stared at him.

He was totally flustered, and he said, "My daughter! I haven't seen her in two days! She was gonna check on the Brewster family. Whatever happened to them might've happened to her."

The sheriff said, "Jesse, I fully understand your concern, but it's best you leave this up to us. The Brewster place is where we're headed first, to see if we can find evidence that'll get us started tracking somebody. I'll tell you the truth, Heck found them wiped out, but Danielle wasn't with 'em. She's probably safe somewhere and we'll probably find her and make sure she *stays* safe."

"I wanna be there when she's found."

"You'll just drag us down. You're a saloon keeper, you've been a townie all your life. We know what we're doin', so let us handle it."

"I can't stand not knowing where she is or what's happening to her."

"I understand, but you've gotta let it be."

"Okay," Jesse said sadly, finally turning away and trudging back toward his saloon.

Sheriff Parkman sidled over to Wild Bill and Calamity Jane and said to Billy, "How's your eyesight gonna hold up?"

He sort of blew the question off, saying, "If we run into a pack of wild Injuns or cannibals, I'll point my gun in the same direction you others are aimin' and blast away at 'em. I don't expect we'll encounter anything much trickier, and if we do, I'll hope to get in close."

"I'll stick by you -- *honey*," Calamity said, busting his chops over that one word. Then she laughed at him, and he laughed too.

The posse members got their horses trotting in a westerly direction out of town, possibly headed into a type of danger they knew little about. They didn't talk much. None of them believed in useless chatter. Action was what counted. They were grimly determined to save all the desperately trapped folks that they could and gun down any beings, alive or dead, that were bent on cannibalizing them.

CHAPTER 33

When Father Ed's party finally trudged out of the wooded clearing, they came upon a cliff with some kind of cave near the top.

The cave looked like a promising place of safety and shelter, but it was up so high it was totally out of reach. To make matters worse, four ghouls were hunkered around the base of the cliff, munching on the remains of recent victims.

"Look at that cave up there," Father Ed said. "If we could drive those misbegotten creatures away and climb up there and barricade it, it'd be almost impregnable."

Dispiritedly, Sister Hillary said, "The only way we might drive them away would be with fire. Rocks and clubs won't faze them. I wish we could've brought torches. I never thought I'd ever say this, but I wish we had guns."

Annie piped up. "How do we know for sure that rocks wouldn't hurt them?"

"You know, Sister Hillary Annie might be right," said Father Ed. "A vicious dog will sometimes yelp and run away if it's hit hard enough with a brick or a stone."

"Yes, and if we toss stones," Sister Hillary shot back at him, "They'll know we're here. At the moment, they're not paying any attention to us, thank God."

Annie said, "They're like my dog, Suzie. When you give her bacon treats, she's so into them she blots everything else out."

"Wisely said," Father Ed told her, putting a hand on her shoulder.

She shuddered as a fearful thought hit her. "Oh my gosh! Suzie's home by herself! What if those things break in?"

Sister Hillary said, "You're assuming they're even around your house, and they may not be, and I don't think they crave any other kinds of animals."

Father Ed asked, "Does your pet have some food and water?"

"I filled up her dog dish before Mom and I left. There's a slot in the back door so she can get out and pee. Oh, geeze! I can't stop wanting to cry about my mom, and what if Suzie gets jumped when she's out in the yard doing her business?"

Annie started to cry, and Sister Hillary put her arm around her and stroked her hair, saying, "There, there, honey. Jesus doesn't give us any cross to carry that's too heavy for us to bear. We'll get through all this somehow, with God's help, and you'll have a long, happy life ahead of you."

CHAPTER 34

A prospector riding a pack-laden mule made his way along a cattle trail. They both had drunk water from a stream, so he felt temporarily refreshed and was gratified that his mule was trudging with more alacrity. He had been panning for gold out of that stream for the past six days, camping out very close to it, guarding it from claims jumpers.

In big bold letters scrawled on a piece of wood, he had given his name and his brief declaration that the claim was his, and he needed to hope no one would go near it till he could make it to Deadwood and come back with legal documentation.

He was eager for his bag of gold nuggets and slivers to be weighed by an assayer who would pay him maybe as much as eight or nine hundred dollars, which was what he had guessed they were worth. He was electrified by the thought that if the claim didn't peter out too soon, he was going to be rich.

But gunshots rang out and he was killed outright and fell dead.

Otarro and four of his Comancheros rode up, their guns smoking, and laughed when they saw the mule standing there, unhurt by the volley.

"That there's one lucky animal," one of the men said. "With all the lead flyin' his way, he oughtta be dead."

Chortling, Otarro sarcastically said, "I'm surprised this here gold miner ain't wearin' one of my brother's fuckin' ghost shirts. Mighta saved him."

They all got a kick out of that. Then one of them said, "Want me to plug the mule?"

"Naw," said Otarro. "He's just a dumb beast. He don't even mind that we're gonna steal his former owner's gold."

CHAPTER 35

Father Ed, Sister Hillary, Annie, and the other kids were still at the bottom of the cliff. Close by, ever a threat, some brain-dead zombies were continuing to feast on human remains, and Sister Hillary was immensely bothered by the fact that she didn't even know who they had been in life, and therefore could not pray for them by name. But she prayed nonetheless for God to have mercy on their souls.

Father Ed was keeping a constant eye on the zombies placidly eating at the base of the cliff, and was also studying the cave above it, considering the fact that there were trees with thick branches close to the edge.

He said, "If we could circle around and get on top, we could lower ourselves into the cave."

"How?" Annie asked.

In spite of her respect and affection for Father Ed, she thought he was starting to pipedream.

He said, "We'd need a strong rope, like a bull rope or something. Even a regular lariat for roping steers."

Sister Hillary said, "We have nothing. We're poorly equipped for survival, Father. We're in good shape for the next world but not this one."

He said, "Don't despair, Sister. God is on our side."

She wasn't sure she still believed that. Bad things happened to good people, and she had never been able to accept any of the Church's reasoning about that.

All of a sudden, gunshots erupted and the ghouls at the foot of the cliff were being killed in a vicious fusillade.

Two of Otarro's men did the killing. Then they stepped out of the woods behind Father Ed, Sister Hillary and the school kids.

Sister Hillary blurted, "Oh! Thank the Lord!"

She blessed herself, immediately viewing the men as saviors. But Father Ed was more stoical, so he just stared at them. He became even more uneasy when he realized their skin was unevenly tanned in the patches that weren't covered with war paint. They wore head bands, feathers, leather breechclouts and armbands, but they were white men underneath their disguises, causing one word to leap into Father Ed's mind -- Comancheros!

His Civil War regiment had to fight off a band of them who had chosen to attack Union soldiers while they were preoccupied by the Confederates. Father Ed knew they were vicious savages who gave no quarter and took no prisoners.

He jerked his head around as more of them -- on horseback -- emerged from among the trees on the far side of the clearing.

The first two, the ones who had killed the ghouls in their opening fusillade, strode quickly toward two wounded ghouls who were trying to get up, and matter-of-factly shot both of them in the head.

Otarro and three more of his men now came forth, out of the woods, on horseback.

Otarro barked, "What've we got *here?*"

He eyed Father Ed's group with malice.

The priest grimaced, realizing that for sure they might be out of the frying pan but into the fire.

He had no doubt it when one of Otarro's henchmen said, "More hostages. More zombie feed, Otarro."

Another henchman said, "More'n we need. We don't wanna have to deal with any more adults, do we?"

Otarro said, "Kneel down and pray, Father. You too, Sister."

Shakily, Father Ed said, "We can't do you any harm. We're poor little lost sheep. Lost to our friends, lost to our loved ones."

He felt ready to give his life, if the Lord wanted him to, but still he thought he needed to live in order to save the children in his care.

Sister Hillary begged, "Please don't hurt the children. We'll do anything you say."

The Comancheros guffawed.

Otarro said, "Maybe your God will protect them from us, Sister -- and from the ghouls. But I doubt it.

Too bad they ain't wearin' some of my brother's ghost shirts."

Because of all the spite he felt toward Nocona, he always made fun of the ghost shirts anytime he got a good chance.

He shouted at Father Ed and Sister Hillary. "Get down on your knees! Now!"

The kids were wailing.

Father Ed and Sister Hillary both knelt and began saying an Act of Contrition.

"Oh, my God, I am heartily sorry for having offended Thee, and I detest all my sins because I dread the loss of heaven and the pains of hell. But most of all because they offend Thee, my God, who are all good and deserving of all my love..."

They didn't get to finish it.

BLAM! BLAM!

Otarro and one of his gang members shot them both in the head and the crumpled to the earth.

Jed and Danielle heard the shots in the distance, glanced at each other, then headed in the direction of the gunfire, along the path they were already on. They had tethered their horses at the entrance to the path rather than trying to force them through dense foliage. On foot, they picked up their pace, then started to run.

It only took them five or ten minutes to burst into the clearing where the cliff was -- but they were too late. The last of the kids, their wrists bound with rope, were being herded into the bed of a wagon.

Jed and Danielle reflexively aimed their rifles in the direction of the wagon, sighting in on what they thought were two Indians -- but they held their fire for fear of hitting the kids. Jed lowered his weapon and motioned for Danielle to do the same, even though he knew by now that he had to be careful not to act like he was giving her orders.

They both watched the wagon as it quickly disappeared into the woods across the clearing.

He said, "Obviously those kids are being kidnapped! We've gotta try and catch up and help them somehow!"

She said, "I think there's a wider road that way! Wide enough for that wagon!"

As they moved deeper into the clearing beneath the cliff, they found themselves standing over the bodies of Father Ed and Sister Hillary, and Danielle burst into tears when she recognized them. She hadn't known them well on a personal level, but she had met them at the school during meetings about funding.

"You knew them?" Jed asked when he saw her crying.

She nodded, and he put his arm around her shoulders.

He said, "Those bastards killed this priest and nun, so they won't hesitate to kill children."

CHAPTER 36

Sheriff Parkman and his group of deputized scouts and gunslingers -- Wyatt Earp, Heck Thomas, Doc Holliday, Wild Bill Hickok, and Calamity Jane -- arrived at the trail below low hills where Red Feather and Bold Eagle were killed, and Nocona was wounded and captured.

They found the decomposing remains of the two Indian Policemen.

The sheriff said, "Don't nobody dismount! We can't help these two now. Hopefully, when all this is over, we can notify the Lakota tribe's leaders to come out and perform whatever their appropriate ceremony is."

Calamity said, "I'd like to give the desperados who did this the proper ceremony -- a bullet in the head or a noose around their necks."

Wyatt said, "My sentiments exactly, honey."

She snapped, "I ain't your goddamn honey! I ain't nobody's honey, not even my husband's."

Wild Bill said, "Now, honey..."

She said, "Shut the hell up!"

Not wanting to see their real business out here get derailed, Heck Thomas said, "Plain to see the two

Indian Police escorts were killed right here, but what'd they do with Nocona?"

Grimly, Sheriff Parkman said, "His twin brother, Otarro, probably took him and skinned him alive by now."

CHAPTER 37

One of Otarro's men was driving the horse-drawn wagon with kids tied up in the bed, and another Comanchero was sitting beside him on the driver's bench. Their two horses were hitched behind the wagon and forced to keep up with it.

Otarro and two other gang members were on horseback on either side of the wagon, but had to drop behind it when the trail got too narrow. But mostly it was wide enough to be passable without anybody needing to drop back.

The wagon driver, known to the other desperados as Freaky Freddy, said, "How much money you think these kiddies are gonna fetch us?"

The henchman riding shotgun was called Flathead Logan because one side of his forehead *was* flat, probably from birthing pressure. He said, "Otarro told me it depends on not just how rich their parents are, but how much they keep on hand in greenbacks and gold coins. But he thinks all the citizens of Deadwood will be anxious to pitch in."

"Well, we'd be in a lot less hassle," Freaky Freddy said, "if we killed all the wee little ones and just kept the Alderson girls. They're the ones we know for sure have rich parents. The rest of 'em probably ain't worth a bucket of piss."

In the back of the wagon, Annie Kimble and three other kids from St. Willard's were tied up along with Becky and Lisa Alderson, the two sisters that Freaky Freddy and Flathead Logan had talked about as having rich parents. They were cute little blondes with big blue eyes, ages seven and eight.

Lisa took a long look at Annie and piped up, "Who're you?"

"My name is Annie. This is Timmy, Alan and Carrie. We're from St. Willard's. We got attacked and burnt out, and we had to run. Then these men showed up looking like Injuns, and we thought they were saving us, but instead, they killed our priest and nun and tied us up."

"I'm Lisa, and this is my sister Becky," Lisa said.

Becky said, "Our parents are rich. Are yours?"

Dejectedly, Annie said, "I don't know where my daddy is, and my mother is dead."

"We have to try to get away," Lisa said urgently. "They captured me and Becky after our dancing lessons before all this other crazy stuff started happening. They think they're gonna get a million dollars from our daddy. They're holding us for ransom, but I'm scared they won't let us go, whether Daddy pays or not. We don't even know if our parents are still alive."

Freaky Freddy and Flathead Logan were listening to all this, and now Flathead yelled over his shoulder at the kids.

"You better *hope* he pays! If he doesn't, you and your sister won't see another sun come up! Unless Otarro makes you join the other little kiddies he call his wives. You cutie-pies prob'ly don't know what sex is, but you'll soon learn."

Flathead and Freaky Freddy brayed with laughter, and Freddy said to Flathead, "I told ya we shoulda gone straight to the Alderson place last night. We coulda hit 'em under the cover of darkness."

Flathead said, "You better stop bitchin' if you know what's good for ya. It was Otarro's call."

CHAPTER 38

Sheriff Parkman led his posse into the clearing where the remains of St. Willard's Church and School were still smoking. With their guns at the ready, they saw ghouls shambling around by the shed or else squatting and eating and fighting over human body parts.

The posse opened fire.

The ones clumped in a group by the shed were easy targets and those were the ones Wild Bill chose.

"Hot damn!" he cried out with glee. "My bad eyes ain't botherin' me nohow! It's like firin' at a family of buffalo! Wherever you point you can't miss, you're gonna bring somethin' *down!*"

Two zombies stepped out from behind the shed, one carrying a severed arm and the other biting into a severed hand. Hickok and Calamity Jane opened fire on them. Calamity's bullet was dead on; it struck the creature carrying the severed arm and it hit the ground hard. But Bill's bullet went into the other zombie's chest even though he was aiming for its head. It dropped the severed hand but other than that, it didn't react much, even though there was now a gaping hole in its chest.

Wyatt said, "Gotta hit 'em in the head, Bill."

"I know that, goddamn it!"

Calamity knew it was an easy shot for her, but she refrained, wanting her husband to have a chance to prove to himself that he wasn't washed up.

He steadied his pistol, squeezed the trigger -- and BLAM! -- it was a clean head shot this time. The zombie hissed and groaned as it fell, and she knew it made Bill feel good, as if he was still the marksman he used to be.

When there were no more zombies in the immediate area, Heck wheeled his horse to face Sheriff Parkman and his mount and said, "I think we got 'em all, so what're we gonna do with 'em? Build a bonfire?"

"Hell no! We're gonna let 'em stay here and rot!"

"Medical schools would love to have at least a couple of them," Doc Holliday ventured to say. "I know my pal when I was in that college in Philly would have wanted to examine them for scrapie -- or anything else of a diagnostic nature."

"Well, if he was here he could've carted a couple of 'em off," Sheriff Parkman said. "I wouldn't have minded in the least. But he ain't here, unfortunately, and we've gotta get a move on if we're gonna rescue anybody."

CHAPTER 39

Otarro's murderous gang plodded on through the woods with the wagon full of captive kids.

Freaky Freddy turned his head and closed his eyes, as if to mitigate the burn in his throat from a slug of whiskey out of Flathead's flask -- and when he opened his eyelids, three ghouls were suddenly standing in the middle of the dirt road. The horses hitched to the wagon reared up, neighing in fear, and Freddy fought to regain control -- then the horses' hooves came down, trampling two of the dead things and knocking the third one aside.

In the back of the wagon the kids were screaming and being tossed around.

The wagon went into a sideways skid, hitting the ghoul who had been knocked aside but was now halfway up again, sending it flying till it smashed sideways into a tree.

Freaky Freddy and Flathead Logan were flung out head first. Freddy hit his head against a boulder, breaking his neck, and Flathead was run over by a wagon wheel.

One of the ghouls lay on the ground like a rag doll, its breath rasping feebly and one of its arms flailing weakly, like an insect half crushed but refusing to die.

Otarro rode up and jerked on his horse's reins, halting it, then looked down at the ghoul writhing on the ground and fired a carefully placed shot between its eyes. Part of its skull was blown away and its movements ceased.

Another Comanchero, named Scalper, rode up and stopped next to Otarro. He said, "Our two guys are as dead as they look."

Otarro snickered. He said, "Look on the bright side. Fewer ways to divvy the loot up. Can you handle the wagon?"

"It ain't no use no more," Scalper said. "One of the axles is broke."

Otarro thought quickly and came up with a callous answer. "We'll ditch all the damned kids and leave 'em right here, tied up. The ghouls will make a good meal out of them."

CHAPTER 40

Sheriff Parkman and his band of gunslingers rode out of the woods and into the clearing at the foot of a cliff.

They stared at the ghoul-ravaged bodies of Father Ed and Sister Hillary.

For a long moment, they didn't know what to do next because they couldn't help being stunned. Then they heard what sounded like children crying in the distance.

They perked up. The crying was coming from the woods beyond the clearing, so they cautiously turned their horses that way.

Little Annie Kimble cried out louder, and they spurred their mounts toward her.

In short order they found Annie and the other kids with their wrists and ankles bound. And they were all tied to the trunks of trees.

Sheriff Parkman, trying his best to comfort them, said, "No need for you kiddies to cry anymore. You're safe now. We'll soon have you untied."

"Who're you?" Annie asked suspiciously.

"I'm Sheriff Parkman. One of the good guys."

Annie blurted, "They left us here to die! They wanted the ghouls to sniff us out! They took two other kids with them, but they left all of *us!* They said 'cause we're too poor to bother with. My name is Annie, and this is Timmy, Alan and Carrie."

"What're the names of the two kids they still have?"

"Becky and Lisa Alderson. Those outlaws looked like they were trying to be like Injuns, but they were White. They think Becky and Lisa's Daddy is rich and is going to pay them a big ransom."

The little boy named Timmy said, "Those bad guys, they killed Father Ed and Sister Hillary. After their wagon crashed is when they took those two rich girls with them and left us to be...to be...*eaten.*" Even saying that last word made him shudder. He clammed up, threw himself down onto his stomach and let the grass muffle his bawling.

Heck Thomas asked Annie, "Do you have any idea where they're heading?"

"Just wherever Lisa and Becky's house is," Annie said. "Mr. Alderson's ranch."

"I know where that is," Heck realized. "I tracked a train robber who holed up near there, about six months ago. Didn't wanna kill him, but I had to. He made me. He fired at me with a little Derringer he kept in his sleeve, and I had to fire back."

"Otarro is the leader of those Injun-looking white guys," Annie said. "I heard him bossing them around and laughing like crazy when he said they'd get a lot of money from Mr. Alderson, then they'd kill the girls and their parents. When is the killing gonna stop, Sheriff Parkman?"

"I wish I knew, honey. we're trying our best, believe me."

Wyatt, and Wild Bill had been looking around up the trail, and now they rode up to the Sheriff, Doc, and Calamity and said, "Their wrecked wagon is up there a piece, the rear axle broken. That's why they ditched these kids and took only the two sisters." There's also a couple dead ghouls and dead Comancheros lying around the wrecked wagon.

"Well, we can't linger," Sheriff Parkman said. "And there's no reason to. We've gotta first find a safe place for the kids here, then hustle over to the Alderson ranch and hope we're in time." He turned in his saddle and addressed everybody who was with him.

"Let's move out quickly! We know what we have to do! People's lives might depend on us!"

CHAPTER 41

A short while after the sheriff's posse departed, Jed and Danielle came upon the scene of the wrecked wagon, without knowing that a posse had been there ahead of them.

They had no idea where the kidnapped kids would be, but they were glad they didn't see any young kids' bodies along with the two dead Comancheros and a couple of what looked like ghouls, shot in their heads.

They were overwhelmed by an eerie silence all around them, then they heard some faint moans coming from some weeds at the side of the dirt road.

They crept up on the source of the moans and found Flathead near death from being run over by a wagon wheel. His chest and abdomen were soaked in blood from being crushed, and one of his arms was broken and jutting at a weird angle.

He moaned and begged for help.

"We can't do anything for you, we don't have any medical supplies," Danielle told him. "And frankly, I don't much care. Why did you have to hook up with a bunch of renegades? Didn't you have any sympathy for those kids you kidnapped?"

"Yeah...I honestly did...but I didn't want to be poor anymore. And Otarro woulda...killed me...if I...tried to buck him."

"Where is he headed with them?" Jed asked sternly.

"The...Alderson ranch...the sisters have...a rich daddy...he's gonna pay..."

"Let's go there!" Danielle said excitedly to Jed.

"Please...don't leave me to die," Flathead said with a weakening voice.

"We can't put you on one of our horses," Jed said, "and there's nowhere we can take you. And even if there was, you'd probably die before we got you there."

He bent low over Flathead to make sure the man was hearing him. But Flathead wasn't hearing anything anymore. His eyes were rolled back in his head, and he wasn't breathing.

CHAPTER 42

Sheriff Parkman and his posse didn't have a coach or a wago, and therefore they had little choice but to hoist each of the four kids up behind four posse member's saddles, to take them to a nearby ranch where he knew the homesteaders.

"Why don't we split up?" Calamity Jane suggested. "You, Heck, Doc and Wyatt take the little kids to safety and me and Billy head to the Alderson place. I know where it is."

"Not a bad suggestion in a way," the sheriff said. "But I don't think that just you and Billy can easily contend with Otarro and his gang. And if we blow it, we put everyone at risk including ourselves."

He was also thinking, but did not want to allude to the fact, that Wild Bill wasn't the marksman he used to be, because of his failing eyesight.

So his original plan was adhered to, in the hope they could make sure that the frightened little kids were well taken care of and still get to the Alderson ranch in time.

By the same token, not knowing that there was a posse at work trying to accomplish the same thing they were, Jed and Danielle got to the Alderson place ahead of them. They believed it was on them as to whether or not the kidnapped kids could be saved. They also believed that the kidnappers were still in possession of all the kids, not just the two sisters.

After tethering their mounts back a ways, they sneaked up to the edge of the vast lawn of the ranch house and peaked from behind trees and shrubbery. They were startled when they saw a half dozen ghouls on the lawn, grouping as if getting ready to attack the house.

One of the ghouls was wearing a security guard uniform.

Jed said, "Look at that one, Danielle. He was probably stationed here to protect the family, but he got himself shot and turned into one of those damned things."

"My God," she whispered. "Will it never end?"

Suddenly, from behind them, they heard heavy footsteps and rasping breath. A ghoul was almost upon them! And this one was also wearing a security guard uniform. He looked as though he was killed by a shotgun blast because part of his chest and the bottom half of his chin had been blown away, and the front of his uniform was a bloody mass of sundered cloth and riddled flesh. A fragment of chin bone and teeth hung uselessly from a relatively intact lower jaw.

The thing reached at Jed, who at the last moment got an arm up to protect himself, but the creature clutched Jed's wrist and landed on top of him, growling hungrily, and trying to bite into him with what remained of his jaw and teeth.

Just in time, Danielle smashed the ghoul's head with a heavy rock -- once, twice, and again.

The ghoul fell with its dead skull busted open, oozing brain matter, then lying still.

Jed scrambled out from under the dead thing and took a moment to collect himself, staring gratefully at Danielle.

But he knew there was no time to waste. He motion to her and said, "C'mon! Quick!"

He ran in a low crouch, with Danielle keeping up with him, and when they reached the mansion-like ranch house, they ducked around one side of it.

They heard a noise and peaked out. The front door had opened, and one of Otarro's men, the one called Scalper, came out onto the porch pointing a rifle and looking all around the front lawn. He appeared to take note of the same cluster of ghouls previously seen by Jed and Danielle.

He turned and went back inside, then he came back out, stooping to drag Mr. Alderson out by his ankles.

Scalper said, "I bet a rich piece of shit like you never dreamed about ending up as zombie feed."

Half whimpering, Mr. Alderson said, "We paid you your ransom. You promised you'd let us go."

"Haw! You're a sucker for believing us!" Scalper said. "Don't you know you should never trust criminals?"

He giggled at his own wit. Then he resumed dragging Mr. Alderson down off the porch and into the yard where the zombies could readily get to him.

But as soon as Scalper got halfway into the yard, Jed sneaked up behind him and smashed him in the head with his rifle butt, and Scalper went down.

With a powerful second blow, Jed bashed Scalper's head in, and Danielle quickly untied Mr. Alderson.

Jed shouted in a hoarse whisper, "Get out of sight around the side of the house, Mr. Alderson! Are your daughters still alive?"

"For the time being. So is my wife. At least I hope so. Please help them."

"That's why we're here. What about the other kids?"

"There are no others-- what do you mean?"

This was puzzling news to Jed, but he had to keep going. Now he really didn't know whether the other kids he had seen were alive or dead.

He motioned to Danielle to stay down and follow him back across the lawn and up onto the porch. They each carried a rifle and had pistols tucked in their belts as they into the house through the door that Scalper had left open when he dragged Mr. Alderson out.

They found themselves in a lavishly appointed Victorian-style living room, where they saw Mr. Alderson's wife bound and gagged in a corner.

Hearing rummaging sounds from upstairs, Jed motioned to Danielle to guard Mrs. Alderson while he crept up the steps.

As he turned a corner at the top of the staircase, the butt of his rifle grazed the wall.

Otarro called out, "That you, Scalper? Did you feed the zombies?"

Jed stepped into the room, pointing his rifle.

Otarro, in the midst of taking jewelry from a jade box and stuffing it into an already bulging pillow case, spun around and went for the revolver in his belt.

Jed fired and the slug hit Otarro in the shoulder.

At the same time Otarro got off a shot that went wild.

Jed's second slug slammed into Otarro's chest, the impact sending him crashing through a bedroom window and through it in a head-first dive down into the yard.

Danielle yelled from downstairs. "Jed! Are you all right?"

"Yeah! I got him!"

"Thank God!"

Jed, who was unwounded, sent to the shattered window and looked down.

Blood trickling from his wounds, Otarro was trying to crawl and get to his feet. But a party of ghouls had him surrounded.

The ghouls closed in.

Otarro tried to fight back, but the hungry ghouls had the upper hand. They swarmed over him, tearing him apart.

Shaken by the grisly end that Otarro came to, Jed backed away from the window. With his rifle ready, he backed out into the hall.

He spied a door half ajar. He kicked the door open and jumped back, half expecting the report of a gun. But nothing happened, and he entered the room. He saw two four-poster beds, and on the beds were the two Alderson girls, Lisa and Becky, each tied and gagged, their arms and legs spread-eagled and roped to the brass rungs. The way they were lying there, it seemed to Jed they may have been raped, and he could not stand letting that thought enter his mind.

They strained to look up at him, and the fear in their faces softened as they saw he was not one of their captors.

He bent over Lisa and untied her gag, then asked her, "Anyone else in the house that I should know about?"

She said, "Our mom and dad, if they haven't been killed." The words came out weak and sad.

"They're alive," Jed told her. "They're gonna be okay."

Shots rang out from outside, and he leapt over to a bedroom window and peeked out.

Sheriff Parkman's posse was on the scene, gunning down ghouls, wheeling their horses this way and that, keeping up a constant barrage. Heck Thomas, Wyatt Earp, Doc Holliday, Wild Bill Hickok and Calamity Jane kept firing relentlessly, trying to make each shot count, sending one ghoul after another toppling to the earth.

Finally, the sheriff and his posse surrounded the house, taking aim at the doors and windows.

Sheriff Parkman commanded, "Don't nobody get trigger-happy! You hear me? Innocent people might be holed up in there!"

Heck Thomas and Wyatt Earp brought their horses up beside the sheriff's and drew beads on the front door.

The sheriff called out, "This is the law! Come out with your hands up!"

Slowly the front door swung the rest of the way open, but whoever had kicked it open hung back.

Wyatt and Heck had their guns cocked.

Sheriff Parkman called out again. "Don't nobody fire!"

Jed came out with his hands up. Then Danielle. Then Mr. and Mrs. Alderson and their two daughters.

Jed shouted to the sheriff, "The Aldersons are shaken, but they're gonna be fine! Their kidnappers are all dead!"

Mrs. Alderson also called out. "Let your men stay here and rest a while, Sheriff! I'm gonna bring out ham sandwiches and beer!"

"I could go for some of that," Wild Bill said. "Wonder if they got any whiskey."

CHAPTER 43

In a far corner of the Aldersons' property, the corpses of the undead were being dragged with ropes and piled up in a heap.

Sheriff Parkman, Wyatt Earp, Heck Thomas, Wild Bill Hickok, and Calamity Jane were all pitching in with the grisly task. So were Jed Harris and Danielle Greer, who stopped every so often to hug each other and trade pecks on their cheeks.

Doc Holliday was resting in the shade of the porch, sitting between the two Alderson daughters, dealing cards, and teaching them how to play gin rummy. He was tired and thought it best that he should not be dragging dead zombies around, for fear of having a coughing fit.

When all the zombies were piled up, they were doused with kerosene by Heck and Hickok. Then Sheriff Parkman used his cigar to light a torch.

He touched the torch to the kerosene and flames leapt high into the summer air.

Billows of black smoke climbed into the clear blue sky.

Everybody watched.

Nobody felt like shouting hooray.

CHAPTER 44

The Ghost dancers were dancing in the traditional circle of worshiping the Great Spirit, writhing and chanting wildly and with smiles on their faces, blessed by their powerful faith that they were helping their ancestors to return.

Nocona sat cross-legged in their midst, wearing his finest, most elegant Ghost Shirt as he took repeated puffs on his ceremonial pipe.

His arm, shoulder and thigh were still bandaged, but healing, thanks to his Lakota gods.

He knew the buffalo herds would soon be back on the plains, the Whites would be gone, and his people would be at peace.

EPILOGUE

This novel, though largely fictional, is also factual in many equally large respects.

It is historically true that Wyatt Earp, Heck Thomas, Wild Bill Hickok and Calamity Jane were all in Deadwood in the time period when the story takes place. Doc Holliday may have been there too, because he and Wyatt really were best friends, and hung around together a lot of the time.

All of the details concerning Doc's career in dentistry are factual. I don't know if he really had any interest in scrapie, which is a real disease that I described accurately, but who's to say he didn't.

There's pretty good historical evidence that Calamity Jane and Bill Hickok were married for a while. Also, there's evidence that Bill suffered from an eye disease that contributed to his later shortcomings as a gunslinger, and may have helped make him vulnerable to the man who shot him in the back while he was playing poker and drew the Dead Man's Hand, aces and eights. He was killed on August 2, 1876, not long after the events of this story took place, which they did, if you choose to believe in them.

Doc Holliday only lived to be thirty-six years old, and died of his tuberculosis. His pal, Wyatt Earp, lived till age eighty, and got to bask in his own fame, which even in his own lifetime, was largely fictional.

Heck Thomas truly was one of the bravest and most fearless United States Marshals in the history of the Old West; he died in 1912 at age sixty-two. It is *not* fiction that he was a scout for the Confederates when he was only thirteen.

I have taken liberties with the time frame of the Ghost Dances. They actually didn't reach their height till the 1880's or a bit later. Nocona and Otarro are fictional, but based on real medicine men of the Lakota, and espousers of the dances.

If there really were flesh-eating zombies in and around Deadwood in the nineteenth century, the facts have been covered up, so I had to improvise. I think it's best if I refrain from saying how much is improvised and how much is true, in case you wish to believe all of it.

For more information on John Russo,
his books, movies, and official merchandise,
please visit:

www.TheJohnRusso.com

ABOUT THE AUTHOR

With 40 books published internationally and 19 movies in worldwide distribution, John Russo has been called "a Living Legend." He began by co-authoring the screenplay for the horror classic, *Night of the Living Dead*, and went on to build an iconic decades-long career.

His books on the art and craft of movie making have become bibles of independent production and have won a national award for Superior Nonfiction. Quentin Tarantino and many other noted filmmakers have stated that Russo's books have helped them launch their careers.

John Russo wants people to know he's "just a nice guy who likes to scare people" -- and he's done it with novels and films such as *Return of the Living Dead, Midnight, The Majorettes, The Awakening, Heartstopper,* and *My Uncle John is a Zombie!* He's had a long, rewarding career, and he shows no signs of slowing down. In 2024, Lionsgate acquired a Western written by him, *The Night They Came Home*, about the murder spree perpetrated by the Rufus Buck gang, who were all hanged in 1895.

Russo's popularity among genre fans remains at a high pitch. He appears at many movie conventions each year as a featured guest, and hundreds of attendees come to his tables or to the bar to share drinks, jokes, and serious conversation.

www.ingramcontent.com/pod-product-compliance
Lightning Source LLC
Chambersburg PA
CBHW070935250626
47159CB00009B/3262